The
gargoyle
at the gates

THE LOST gargoyle SERIES

THE
GARGOYLE
AT THE GATES

THE LOST GARGOYLE SERIES

BY

PHILIPPA

DOWDING

DUNDURN
TORONTO

Editor: Allister Thompson
Design: Courtney Horner
Printer: Webcom

Library and Archives Canada Cataloguing in Publication

Dowding, Philippa, 1963-
        The gargoyle at the gates / Philippa Dowding.

Issued also in electronic formats.
ISBN 978-1-4597-0394-0

        I. Title.

PS8607.O9874G36 2012   jC813'.6   C2012-902129-6

        3   4   5   16   15   14   13

We acknowledge the support of the **Canada Council for the Arts** and the **Ontario Arts Council** for our publishing program. We also acknowledge the financial support of the **Government of Canada** through the **Canada Book Fund** and **Livres Canada Books**, and the **Government of Ontario** through the **Ontario Book Publishing Tax Credit** and the **Ontario Media Development Corporation**.

Care has been taken to trace the ownership of copyright material used in this book. The author and the publisher welcome any information enabling them to rectify any references or credits in subsequent editions.

J. Kirk Howard, President

Printed and bound in Canada.

Visit us at
Dundurn.com | @dundurnpress | Facebook.com/dundurnpress | Pinterest.com/dundurnpress

Dundurn 3 Church Street, Suite 500 Toronto, Ontario, Canada M5E 1M2	Gazelle Book Services Limited White Cross Mills High Town, Lancaster, England LA1 4XS	Dundurn 2250 Military Road Tonawanda, NY U.S.A. 14150

For my brother Christopher,
who created the tin foil fairy

PROLOGUE

The year is 1936.

A young boy and an old man are sitting together, side by side, on a rock in a churchyard. It's a lovely place, with an old apple orchard and a small river running along between the trees and the church courtyard.

An ancient lion statue stands nearby, regal in the gentle summer evening.

The boy and the man are very still, almost as though they are waiting for something. If you listen closely, you can hear the man whispering to the boy:

"They are very shy. You must be extremely quiet, but they will come. They love the apples at this time of year."

The boy's eyes are open wide, and he dares not move his head lest he scare their mysterious visitors away. He is staring straight ahead at the stone lion, long enough to realize that its left ear is broken off and is lying in the grass at its feet. The boy's grandfather gives him a gentle nudge and whispers, "Shhh. See, over there, in the treetops."

The boy squints, hardly daring to breathe. It is difficult to see much in the gathering darkness. The treetops are still ... then suddenly he sees a movement. A leathery claw reaches out from the green leaves of an apple tree and plucks a fruit from the branch. In another tree nearby, a second claw slowly clutches an apple, then in a third tree, a third claw reaches out.

"There are THREE of them?" the boy whispers.

"Here, yes."

The boy considers this. "There are more, then?"

The old man nods. "There may be more ... perhaps."

"Then where are the others?"

The old man shakes his head and shrugs. "Lost. Gone. No one knows for sure."

The boy has many, many more questions he'd like to ask, but he is cut short. In the next moment, a half-eaten apple whizzes through the air and lands at his feet. The boy looks at it, amazed, but doesn't have a chance to say anything, because just then three wondrous creatures emerge from the trees and waddle slowly toward him.

His grandfather has told him they exist, but his grandfather is also known for making up stories.

The boy sits still, barely breathing, until the first creature reaches them and says something in a voice that sounds like gravel, or like pennies swishing in the bottom of a bucket, or maybe like the wind rustling in the winter leaves.

"Snarthen bellatro?" it says, glaring at the boy and his grandfather. It is large and dark, with a ram's head and curly horns.

But the boy hears the gargoyle say something else in its whispery voice, as well. It sounds quite clearly like, "And who are *you*?"

CHAPTER ONE
ON THE WAY TO SCHOOL

It was raining. Again.

Christopher Canning pulled on his muddy rain boots and waited at the door for his many-assorted-older-brothers and his slightly-older-sister to get ready for school. Marbles, the family's large dog, bumped gently into Christopher's leg.

He patted Marbles slowly.

Christopher leaned against the cool door frame and looked across the driveway. Next door to their house, a spiky iron fence surrounded a little park that had gateposts and a locked gate.

He had noticed the park but hadn't examined it. He and his family had just moved into this house a few weeks earlier. He hadn't looked around yet, not on his own, not without his many-assorted-older-brothers-and-slightly-older-sister tagging along.

It was an interesting-looking park. It had a stone fountain, and the water made a gentle bubbling sound. In the centre of the fountain were two entwined seahorses, perched on their tails. The water sprayed out of their horns and splashed into the stone bowl beneath them.

There was a small apple tree, too, but apart from that and a few benches and bushes, not much else. It was odd, not a park for playing in, since there were no swings or slides or any playground equipment.

No, not for playing in. But for what then?

Christopher decided it might be for sitting quietly in. That would be the most special thing of all, as far as he was concerned. Somewhere quiet to sit and think, alone. As if on cue, and to remind him of their constant existence, his many-assorted-older-brothers-and-slightly-older-sister (there were five Canning children in all) entered the hallway and started jostling for their raincoats and boots.

"Move it, C.C.," Marc (his oldest brother) said as he gently pushed Christopher aside to get at the boots.

"Here's your lunch, C.C.," said Claire (his slightly-older-sister), handing him a lumpy paper bag. He slipped it into his backpack and stepped out of the crowded hallway onto the front porch of the house.

He leaned against the porch railing and again stared at the little park. A red-and-yellow streetcar rattled by, filled with people going downtown to work and school.

He and his brothers and sister were all walking to their new schools. The eldest Cannings were going to the high school, and he was going to the junior school. He was used to new schools, since he and his family moved all the time. His dad and mom worked for different parts of the government — he wasn't sure which parts exactly — so they moved a lot.

His loud family came out of the house and joined him on the porch, popping open umbrellas and stepping out into the rain like one brightly-coloured, many-headed monster. His sister grasped him firmly by the hand and popped her umbrella open over their heads.

"Claire, honestly, I'm twelve years old! I'm too old to hold your hand!" Christopher wailed, trying to pull his hand free, but it was no use. Claire had a vice-like grip and didn't care about mortifying her little brother.

"Come on C.C., it's not that bad!" she said, almost happily. "Great rainy weather for your third awful day at school!" His sister was altogether too happy, most of the time. So downright chipper, it really wasn't natural for a teenager. She pulled him much too cheerfully along the rainy street. As the youngest, he was used to being dragged along by someone at the back of the crowd of many-assorted-older-brothers-and-slightly-older-sister.

But Christopher had noticed that being at the back often had its advantages. You got to see things that people at the front didn't, for instance.

That's why, as Claire dragged him much too happily through the rain to school and past the little park next to their house, he was the only one to notice the gargoyles at the park gates. There were two gateposts with a smallish gargoyle perched on each one. The gargoyles looked very wet and dark.

Rainwater was pouring down their leathery backs and shiny wings, and steam was curling off them in little wisps.

As he passed the gargoyles, he looked up. They had leathery faces and intriguing pouches at their sides. They were perched on the gateposts like cats, with their claws in front of them. They didn't look exactly alike, either, which was interesting. He would have liked to look at them longer, but his sister said, "Hurry up, C.C., honestly, you're such a dawdler."

He liked the look of the gargoyles, so he smiled at them before Claire yanked him away.

That was why he didn't see the first gargoyle stick its tongue out at him.

Or the second gargoyle smile back.

Chapter Two
The Apple Bitten

Christopher made it through day three at his new school. The teacher was assigning their math homework for the evening. "Be sure to practise your multiplication up to the fifteen times tables."

A girl two desks down groaned and slammed her book shut. Her friend, a girl named Kathleen or something, looked gloomy.

The teacher dismissed the class and they all filed out into the hallway. Christopher grabbed his backpack then headed down the old marble stairs and out the front door. As he stood at the streetcar stop, one of his classmates joined him. It was the girl named Kathleen, or something.

They were the only two people at the stop. He looked up at the sky and started rocking back and forth on his feet. He did that whenever he was nervous. Christopher was good at new schools, he'd been to so many. Making new friends, though? Well, that was something different.

The girl turned toward him, clearly trying to think of something to say. Finally she said, "You're ... Christopher, right?"

"Uh-huh. Christopher Canning. My family calls me C.C. for short." He said this so quickly he wasn't sure the girl understood him. Christopher rubbed the top of his shoe against his calf then pushed his glasses up his nose. The girl could see he wasn't going to say anything else.

"I'm Katherine. Newberry," she said, smiling a little. "Nobody calls me K.N., though. Just Katherine."

"Oh. Hi," Christopher said. It was all he could think of. He vowed then and there to start paying more attention to how his sister Claire started such easy conversations with strangers.

The streetcar rattled to a stop and opened its doors. They got on and found seats near the back. The streetcar rattled on its way again.

Katherine got out her notebook and started doing math. Christopher stared out the window. Katherine was saying quietly to herself, "Fifteen times eight. Fifteen times eight," and tapping the pencil on her chin.

"One hundred and twenty," Christopher blurted out.

"What?" she said, surprised.

"One hundred and twenty. Fifteen times eight, it's one hundred and twenty," he said, pointing to her math book. "Oh!" She gave a little smile and wrote down the number in her book. "Okay, what's fifteen times nine? Quick!"

"One hundred and thirty-five," Christopher answered immediately. Katherine scribbled.

"Fifteen times ten?"

"One hundred and fifty." Katherine scribbled again.

"Fifteen times eleven?"

"One hundred and sixty-five." Another scribble.

"And fifteen times twelve?"

"One hundred and eighty."

Katherine wrote down the last answer, slammed her math book shut, and jammed it back into her backpack. "Thanks!"

They were nearing his stop. It was just past an old pub and a tiny library, in front of a bright-red store with a green door, called "Candles by Daye." There was an extra "e" on "Daye," which was kind of funny, but he wasn't quite sure why.

"Well, see you," he said, getting to his feet.

Katherine got up and swung her backpack onto her shoulder. "It's my stop, too. See you later," she said, then pushed open the streetcar doors and stepped onto the sidewalk. She walked ahead of him then disappeared into Candles by Daye. As the store door opened, he heard a little bell ring, and for a second he caught the heavy scent of cinnamon. The door shut and it was quiet again. He stared for a moment at the shop window filled with candles shaped like skulls, dragon statues, and yoga books, but he caught Katherine looking at him through the glass, and he quickly looked away.

Christopher was alone. He looked across

the street. His huge old house was waiting, but everyone was still at work or school. His parents' car wasn't in the driveway, and there were no brothers or slightly-older-sister reading on the front porch. He crossed the street at the crosswalk and found himself standing in front of the locked iron gates of the little park. There was no one around, not even cars passing by, and he was alone except for an old man with a dark coat, a hat, and thick glasses sitting on a bench way down the sidewalk.

The gargoyles were perched on the gateposts above the locked gate. He studied them for a moment. He looked into the locked park, at the stone seahorse fountain bubbling away, and the inviting benches just out of his reach, then back up at the gargoyles. They were dripping wet and very dark and shiny looking. There were little wisps of steam coming off them.

Then he realized that one of the gargoyles was clutching an apple in its claw.

And someone had taken a *bite*.

Chapter Three
Of Marbles and Apple Cores

Who would take a bite out of an apple and stick it in the gargoyle statue's claw?

Christopher wondered if one of his many-assorted-older-brothers-and-slightly-older-sister was playing a trick on him (a real possibility). He was just about to investigate more closely when he heard loud barking from his house next door. He'd forgotten about his dog! He had to take Marbles for a walk! The dog had spotted him standing at the park gates and was going crazy inside the house at the living room window.

"See you later, gargoyles," he said as he turned away. Just then a loud streetcar rattled by, which is why he couldn't be positively sure of what happened next. It might have been someone playing a trick, but he was sure he heard a strange, whispery voice say, "Bellatro smethen sawchen."

Which in itself didn't mean anything.

But Christopher heard the whispery words and a different meaning at the same time, which translated roughly to something like, "DO NOT throw the apple at that boy."

It sounded like the wind whispering in the long summer grass, or like a language that he was just beginning to forget. But he was sure he caught words there, too.

He whipped around and looked at the gargoyles once again, his eyes wide under his glasses. They were just gargoyles, stone figures staring straight ahead. He peered for a few moments then shook his head. He took off his glasses, rubbed his eyes and looked again, but finally decided he must have imagined it. The barking next door was getting more frantic. He had to go.

A few moments later Christopher opened the front door and was inside his house, trying to keep Marbles from knocking him off his feet.

"Yes, I'm happy to see you too, Marbles. Yes, I *will* take you for a walk, just let me get something to eat."

At the word "walk," Marbles started doing a hilarious dance on his front paws. He was a big, spotted dog, so it was a little hazardous to be around him when he was doing his "I'm-going-for-a-walk" dance. Christopher went into the kitchen, grabbed a banana, pocketed Marbles' favourite orange rubber ball, and was about to lift the dog leash off the hook beside the back door, when …

… *whack*!

Something hit the outside of the door, hard, just on the other side of his head. Carefully he opened the door and peered outside.

There was an apple coming to rest at his feet.

And there was a bite out of it!

Christopher looked over at the gargoyles on the park gates. He could just make out the two statues perched dripping wet on the gateposts.

He took off his glasses and rubbed his eyes. He peered through the drizzle and scratched his head. He must be imagining things.

He took Marbles for a walk.

But he was beginning to think there might be something a little *odd* about that park.

Chapter Four
The English Garden: Septimus

James leaned over the book resting on his knee and pushed his dark, curly hair out of his eyes. He was sitting on a bench under an apple tree loaded with fruit. It was a beautiful summer day, and his grandfather's garden was bursting with life. The daisies, asters, and hollyhocks were all in full bloom and filled with bees. Their droning was making James sleepy, but he didn't want to sleep.

He looked over at his grandfather's little thatched cottage and smiled: he really was in *England!* A few months earlier, no one even knew he HAD a grandfather living in England, not even his mother. She was quite surprised (and puzzled) when the letter came with her name on it, inviting James to visit for the summer.

"But you don't *have* a grandfather living in England," she had said, scratching her head. "My father was an odd recluse who disappeared when I was little."

A few phone calls set that straight. Apparently James's grandfather was alive and quite well and wanted to meet his only grandson. (He wanted to meet his only daughter too, but it was going to take some time for James's mother to get used to the idea.)

James had never been anywhere, so after much begging and insisting and reasoning by him and more phone calls and checking by his parents ... he was allowed to go.

So James DID have a grandfather. As for the odd recluse part ... that was turning out to be just a little bit true.

James turned back to his book. A fountain was bubbling quietly nearby, adding to the drowsy atmosphere. Occasionally a bullfrog croaked sleepily from the pond.

There were a few statues in the garden as well, in various states of completion. In one spot, a half-finished frog statue had big eyes and front legs, but its body and back legs had not yet emerged from its stone cradle. In another shady part of the garden, an enormous apple stood proudly half-formed in a squat block of pink stone.

It was a beautiful, eccentric old garden, with the hand of its creator visible in everything.

And it was a sleepy place. James caught himself falling into a doze and sat up straight. He was a little old to be taking afternoon naps, since he was almost sixteen.

He put his chin in his hand and tried to concentrate on his reading. His grandfather had given him a book to read: *A History of Stonemasons in Europe*. It was an interesting book. Stonemasons worked with knives and hammers and saws and made some really important things out of stone, like churches, bridges, castles, and sometimes artistic carvings, including statues and strange gargoyles.

It was fascinating reading, but for some reason he wasn't able to concentrate. The bees and the flowers and the aroma of apples warming in the sun were making his eyelids very heavy.

Just as he was about to doze off again, an apple tree leaf gently fluttered down from the branch above his head and landed with a loudish *flup* onto the page of his open book. It brought him back to his senses.

He brushed the leaf off the page and continued reading. He flicked a bee away from his ear and scratched his nose. A moment later, another leaf softly floated down from the tree and landed on the page with another *flup*.

He brushed it off, darted a peek into the tree above, and went back to his book.

But not for long.

A few seconds later, four or five leaves gently fluttered down onto his book, then more and more. Finally, a steady torrent of leaves poured down upon him, covering both him and his book in a leafy green coat. He gave up trying to read and sat still as the leaves kept coming. He was slowly being buried in a mountain of green apple tree leaves. In moments, only his head was visible, peeking from the top of the mound. James shook his head to remove leaves from his hair and sighed.

He looked up into the tree, and said patiently, "Septimus, if that's you, you're interrupting my reading." A loud giggle erupted from the tree, and then silence. James tried not to smile. It was a deliciously naughty giggle.

"Grampa Gregory, the gargoyles are restless! Septimus is dropping leaves on me!" James called from the leaf pile. An old man poked his head around the side of the garden shed and nodded. He was wearing a floppy green velvet hat that wobbled dangerously, huge leather gloves, and giant, bug-like goggles.

"They're easily bored, James. Do you play any instruments?" the old man called.

"No," James answered, surprised.

His grandfather was holding an enormous chisel and a huge stone hammer. All afternoon James had heard the chisel occasionally hitting stone. His grandfather was working on another half-finished statue (this one looked like it was going to be a spray of wildflowers, asters perhaps).

"Oh, well, try singing to them then," James's grandfather said matter-of-factly, then turned back to his sculpture.

Singing? What would he possibly sing? Clearly his grandfather wasn't going to help him with Septimus.

James shook himself from head to toe and sent the leaves scattering, brushing them from his shoulders and hair. He and his friends used to play in piles of autumn leaves at home. The memory made him smile a little as he went back to his reading.

But not for long. Another leaf fluttered down from the tree....

Chapter Five
Park Serenade

That night after dinner (which was always very noisy and interesting at the Canning house), Christopher was sitting in his bedroom at the top of the house.

Bedrooms were important for Christopher. As the youngest of a large family that moved all the time, he never knew what his next bedroom would be like.

Whenever they moved into a new house, bedrooms were chosen by names drawn from a hat. Christopher had never won the best bedroom in his whole life …

… except this time! Christopher had the *best room* he'd ever seen. It was an octagon, an eight-sided turret at the top of the house, and it had an enormous bay window that faced the little park next door. Everyone had wanted the turret bedroom at the top of the house, but HE was the one whose name was picked. HE won it, it was HIS!

The best part of all was that it was quiet. His many-assorted-brothers-and-slightly-older-sister all had bedrooms on the floors below.

He jumped on his bed and stuck his elbows on the windowsill. He pushed the old windows open as wide as he could. The rain had stopped, and the air was sharp and clean. It was a beautiful autumn evening. He looked down into the park, listening to the water bubbling in the seahorse fountain. From the window he could see the entire park surrounded by the fence, with the bushes, apple tree, and benches in the middle. It wasn't a very big park at all.

He picked up his guitar. He was actually getting pretty good.

He played a song called "Piece Ensemble." It had a nice melody, but it was a bit sad-sounding. When he finished, he laid his guitar against his knee, and looked down into the park.

It was empty.

Then why did he hear someone down there *clapping*?

Chapter Six
Christopher Canning at the Gates

Clapping? What the heck was going on down there?

Christopher glanced over at his desk clock: 7:15 p.m. He could take Marbles out for a walk. The sun was just going down behind the big city buildings in the distance, so it wouldn't be completely dark for another half an hour or so.

He dashed downstairs. His family was finishing up the dinner dishes.

"Mom! I'm taking Marbles for a walk!" he called. Marbles did his "I'm-going-for-walk-dance" while Christopher got the leash and pocketed the orange ball (which was very brave, since it was still gooey and dripping with dog slime).

Boy and dog slipped out the back door into the fresh air. Christopher took a moment to listen to the city noises. He could hear the fountain bubbling in the park, a streetcar rattling along the tracks nearby, and a police siren downtown. Marbles listened, too.

Christopher walked quietly across the driveway beside the house and in a few short steps was leaning against the iron railing of the park fence. All was still except the gently bubbling fountain.

"Let's walk around it, boy." Christopher wasn't sure why, but he was whispering. He and Marbles walked around the park fence in a few moments. It was the smallest park he had ever seen. He was looking for a break in the fence or some easy way into the park, but he didn't find one — the fence was solid all the way around. Someone was smoking a pipe nearby; he could smell strong smoke. He looked, but no one was around.

"Hmm. That's weird. Smell that, boy? Pipe smoke." As if in answer, Marbles sniffed then sneezed. He always sneezed when someone was smoking.

Christopher stopped on the sidewalk in front of the gates and peered inside. He could see the bubbling seahorse fountain. Bushes. Benches. Apple tree. All quiet. No people. Marbles was sniffing at the gateposts and getting all shivery and excited.

"What is it, Marbles?"

Marbles stood on his hind legs and propped his front legs halfway up the gatepost. His black nose was moving a mile a minute — he could smell something really interesting. He couldn't take his eyes off the gargoyle sitting at the top of the gatepost.

Marbles barked and started jumping on his back legs, staring up at the statue, just like he did when he chased a squirrel up a tree. "Calm down, crazy dog. It's made of stone, see?" Christopher reached up as high as he could and was just able to reach the gargoyle. He knocked on its scaly feet. It sounded rock solid and hurt his knuckles.

Marbles calmed down just a little and sat on the sidewalk looking up at the gargoyle, tense as a bowstring.

"I'm going in, but you have to stay here." Christopher snapped Marbles' leash to the gate. Marbles started whining.

"Shhh! I'll be right back." Christopher took a large breath and turned to face the iron railing of the gate. He sucked in his stomach. He turned his head toward the street and eased first his arm, then his leg, then his shoulder through the bars. Moving very slowly and carefully, he squeezed through the iron bars, his head the last thing through. He just made it. He was standing inside the locked park while Marbles whined and shivered outside on the sidewalk.

"Quiet, boy. Keep a lookout for me." Marbles licked his lips and wiggled his tail.

It was odd, but as soon as Christopher entered the park, he felt like everything went quiet. He could see the street through all the bushes, but any sounds of streetcars or sirens were oddly muffled by them. It was very serene and he suddenly felt sleepy, since the bubbling of the fountain sounded soothing and soft. He walked over to it and looked around.

There were no pennies or anything but water in the bowl at the bottom of the fountain. Obviously, no one ever came in here. He'd been to the Queen Elizabeth fountains in Vancouver, and they were always filled with shiny coins from tourists and visitors. He thought that even small, out-of-the-way fountains usually had money in them.

But this fountain was completely coin-free. No visitors in here then. The gates must be locked most of the time, or maybe all of the time?

Christopher took a few more steps and was standing next to the little apple tree, which was not too much higher than his head. It didn't look like it could have been there very long, and yet it was loaded with apples. It was practically glowing, and the fruit hanging on the branches was heavy and golden and smelled magnificent. They were the best apples he'd ever smelled. He took a deep breath. They smelled absolutely perfect, like apples were supposed to smell if you were going to describe them to someone who had never seen or smelled one before.

The scent of the tree was almost overpowering.

Christopher raised his hand and was just about to pick an apple when he heard a whispery voice say, "Forthen grem sawchen?"

It sounded a lot like a winter wind rustling in the trees, or like a language at the very edge of his memory. But at the same time, he also heard the voice say, "Are you stealing that apple, thief?"

He gasped and whirled around, but there was no one. Christopher wanted to run, but his legs wouldn't move. He was stuck to the spot, his heart beating like a hammer in his chest. He stared into the bushes, but there was nothing to see. Just bushes. He forgot to breathe.

Which is why he was able to hear another, closer, sweeter voice say very clearly, "Bellatro smethen dor."

Which sounded a lot like, "Let the boy be."

ZING! Suddenly an apple flew at Christopher out of the bushes. He bolted back to the gates, trying to squeeze through the iron railing as fast as he could.

ZING! ZING! Two more apples narrowly missed his head.

"HEY!" he yelped, but he didn't dare look back.

ZING! Another apple whizzed past his ear. The apple-thrower was toying with him. Christopher could tell that the thrower was very carefully missing him with each shot.

He contorted himself and desperately squeezed through the bars, gasping for air back on the sidewalk. Apples rang loudly against the park side of the gates.

Christopher grabbed his dog's leash and ran. His mother was opening the back door to call him inside just as he reached the house. She had to jump aside to avoid being knocked over by her son as he dashed through the door.

"Christopher, what's wrong?" she called as he ran by her. But he was already at the top of the house, slamming the door to his room.

She looked down at Marbles, who was waiting patiently at her feet, slowly wagging his tail. His leash was still attached, wet and muddy with dank park leaves.

Chapter Seven
The English Garden: Theodorus

James and his grandfather were sitting under an enormous outdoor umbrella, with a sea of newspapers spread out on the table before them. The old man had a huge leather bag stamped with gold letters and symbols at his feet, overflowing with papers, photographs, and newspaper clippings. The afternoon sun was so bright that James was getting a headache. He had his head in his hands as he turned yet another newspaper page.

"Grampa Gregory, what am I looking for again, exactly?" he asked.

His grandfather didn't raise his head from the paper he was reading with the help of a giant magnifying glass. Today the old man was wearing a strange purple corduroy suit and a floppy purple hat to match. James had the sense it was a costume from several centuries ago, almost like something that a swordsman or musketeer might have worn. He wasn't wearing the bug-like goggles though, which was a nice change.

"I've told you! We're looking for what's lost! We need evidence, clues, any mention of anything unusual … gargoyles …" he answered, muttering and trailing off as he went back to his magnifying glass and the newspaper.

"Well, couldn't we just search the Internet?" James immediately regretted his question.

His grandfather glared at him. "YOU can, if you want to, but don't let anyone know what you're searching for. No one is going to find ME on that thing."

Oh yeah. James had forgotten that. His grandfather hated computers, mail, and even distrusted the telephone. James wasn't supposed to let anyone else know what he and his grandfather were doing all summer. No one was to know that they were looking for stories about statues, and in particular anything about gargoyles. Not even James's parents were supposed to know. Whenever they called from Toronto to check on how his summer visit was going, James said everything was fine.

And it *was* fine. James was enjoying his summer trip to England; he just wished he could see more of it before he had to go back home.

He turned back to the newspaper and sighed. After a while he said, "Here's an article about fountains in Florence … they're doing something to one of them. Renovating the statues. Or re-facing the masonry or something. No mention of gargoyles, though." He handed the paper over to his grandfather, who cleaned the magnifying glass on a rag and carefully pored over the page.

James got up and yawned. "I'm taking a walk, I'll be back," he said. He wandered to the green garden pond and sat in the shade of a climbing rose bush. It was definitely cooler in the shade. He took off his sandals and leaned back, yawning again. The pond had lily pads with frogs lurking under them, doing their best to stay cool. He was dozing a little, listening to the water tumble from a fountain nearby when suddenly …

… a splash of water from the pond hit him right in the face. James jumped to his feet, spluttering and wiping away the pond muck.

A large gargoyle broke the surface of the pond, stomped through the water and clambered out. Pond water ran off the gargoyle's dark back and pooled at its taloned feet. It shook its wings a lot like a dog would, spraying more water across the boy. The gargoyle had a heavy body, a head shaped like a ram with curly horns, and stood quite tall (for a gargoyle). The ground shook a little when it stomped across the flagstones, leaving huge, wet gargoyle footprints as it went.

"Hey! Theodorus! You just drenched me in pond water!" James spluttered, backing away.

"Gremice elba," the creature said with a deep, booming laugh, which James heard as "Time to wake up!" It headed off into the apple orchard, still laughing, long arms drooping at its sides.

But before the gargoyle disappeared, James heard it quite clearly say in its strange, whispery voice, "You looked hot."

The gargoyle was right, James WAS hot. It was impossible not to smile, just a little. He decided he might just go for a swim.

Chapter Eight
First Toronto, Now This

Christopher spent that night far away from his window, trying not to look into the park down below. He didn't know what happened in that park, but he did know one thing: he wasn't going back in there.

There was *something*, or maybe several *somethings*, hiding in the bushes. Last he checked, bushes didn't talk, and apples didn't just fling themselves off trees at people.

At least not so you felt like target practice.

It was creepy. He wasn't sure about this new city at the best of times. When his mom and dad had gathered the family together to tell them they were leaving Vancouver and moving to Toronto, he wasn't all that excited about it. He loved Vancouver. He had friends there, it was home.

Everything was different in Toronto. And now he discovered that strange voices spoke in the bushes in Toronto city parks. And not just parks far away in some other part of the city. He heard them in *his* park, right next door to *his* house.

He had a sleepless night, tossing and turning. He kept dreaming that something in the park was howling at the moon. Once he heard a *whack* as something small and hard — an apple? — banged into his bedroom window. He dug his head as deeply as he could under his pillow, but the howling continued all night long.

The next morning, when he had to walk past the park gates on his way to school, he kept his eyes down and *did not* look inside. It was raining, and the gargoyles were spitting water onto the sidewalk, something he didn't remember from the day before. He didn't look up and smile at the gargoyles. He'd never look at them or the park again as far as he was concerned. Claire smiled in surprise when Christopher took her hand as they walked past the gates and didn't let go until they got to his school.

In class that afternoon, Christopher was paired up with Katherine to write a one-page article about their neighbourhood. It was supposed to help all the kids find out who lived closest to them.

The topic was: *What I love most about my part of the city.*

Christopher scratched his nose and fiddled with his pencil as Katherine started writing. He eventually blurted out, "I don't really know the neighbourhood very well, since I've only lived there for a few weeks, so it's not really fair ... to you."

"It's okay," Katherine said, scribbling furiously. "I don't really live in that part of town either. I just visit Candles by Daye in the afternoon after school."

"What are you writing then?" Christopher asked.

"I'm writing about the public library a few doors down from Candles by Daye. It's tiny, but it has a great rooftop garden, with a miniature apple tree and a goldfish pond, and flowers."

"Yeah, I saw it last week. It *is* nice," Christopher said half-heartedly.

Katherine considered for a moment. "Well, there must be *something* you like?"

"I like my bedroom. It's a turret at the top of the house."

Katherine shook her head. "No good. It can't be about anything inside your house. Has to be outside."

They both fell silent. "I don't mind the park in the ravine, that's nice. It's got trees and my dog likes it. That's okay, I guess," he finally said.

Katherine wrote that down. "We need a little more. Anything else you like? Think!"

Christopher shrugged. "I can tell you what I *don't* like: that creepy little park next to my house, it's haunted or something." Katherine jerked her head up and gasped. She dropped her pencil at the same time, too, which surprised Christopher. He jumped up, banged his knee on the bottom of the desk, and started hopping up and down. The teacher came over and asked what was going on.

"Nothing. Sorry, I dropped my pencil," Katherine said. Christopher's eyes were watering, so all he could do was nod.

When the teacher was gone, Katherine stood up and faced Christopher. The classroom was busy with kids talking and chattering, so no one noticed.

She stood over him. "Listen, Christopher Canning or C.C. or whatever you want to be called, that park is *off limits*. Just don't go in there, okay? It's not safe for … you. You're right. It's … haunted … or something. So just stay out!" Katherine was talking in a low whisper, but for some reason, Christopher was very afraid of her. There was something urgent and upsetting in her tone. Her fists were clenched on her hips, and she looked menacing. He glanced over and saw the teacher coming their way again.

He nodded quickly. "Okay … yeah, okay, Katherine, no problem. The park is off-limits, I get it. Don't worry, I won't be going back in there, not after last night. It's okay."

Katherine saw the teacher heading their way too and dragged Christopher down into the seat beside her. The teacher veered away to another noisy group. Katherine finished writing in silence, handed the paper in to the teacher, then went back to her own desk. She didn't look at Christopher again, and she wasn't at the streetcar stop after school.

Christopher stood at the stop by himself, rocking back and forth on his heels.

Katherine had said the park *was* haunted. *Haunted*. Or *something*. She seemed almost panicked that he was going to go back in there, but Christopher definitely didn't get the feeling she was worried about him. No. She was worried about something else.

What could it be?

She said it was "off limits" and to "stay out."

But *why*?

Chapter Nine
The Orange Ball Rolled

For the next few days, Christopher steered clear of the park, except to notice that people hardly ever went in there. Occasionally, city workers opened the gates and went in to rake up leaves or tend to the fountain. Once in a while they even sat in there having their lunch. But apart from them, and an old man with thick glasses, a white straw hat, and a heavy brown coat who sometimes sat on a bench on the sidewalk past the gates, the park was deserted.

Christopher kept his head down when he walked past and made sure his windows were shut carefully every night, although he didn't hear any more howling. Whenever he took Marbles for a walk, they went the long way to the ravine, and he crossed the street far away from the park.

He stayed away from Katherine, too.

He and Katherine managed a polite truce at the streetcar stop, but she wasn't there every day. Christopher tried to forget about the *somethings* in the park, and he almost managed it …

… until one day after school, when he and his many-assorted-older-brothers were playing ball hockey on the driveway beside their house. The driveway was perfect for ball hockey, since it was so long and straight. Christopher wasn't crazy about playing goalie, but as the youngest he never had much say. He was almost *always* the goalie. His oldest brother, Marc, passed the ball to his second-oldest brother, Nathan, who passed it to his third-oldest brother, Adam, who took a slap shot from halfway down the driveway. It went wild, and the bright orange ball bounced off Christopher's goalie mask, whipped through the air, and flew over the spiked iron rails of the park.

The ball rolled deep into the park bushes.

"Nice going, C.C.!" Marc yelled at him.

Christopher took off his mask and dropped his goalie gloves on the driveway. "Now what?" he asked, looking nervously at the park.

"Go get it! You let it fly over the fence!" Adam called.

"No way, you took the slap shot. *You* go get it!" Christopher yelled back.

"Nice try, C.C. The last one who touches it has to find it," Nathan said. He had Christopher there — the last-touch rule *was* ball-hockey law.

It was no use. Marc, Nathan, and Adam had already lost interest in the game and were leaning their hockey sticks against the house. It was almost dinner time anyway. Christopher looked back at the park.

Nothing moved.

He bit his lip. What to do? Everyone bigger than him had gone inside. It was his best ball-hockey ball. It was Marbles' favourite ball. He really didn't want to lose it.

He was putting the goalie equipment and the net away in the shed at the back of the house when he looked over at the park again. The bushes were rustling.

An orange ball shot through the iron bars, crossed Christopher's driveway …

… and rolled to a stop right at his feet.

CHAPTER TEN
THE GIANT AT THE GATES

Christopher gulped, then reached down and picked up the ball.

Something wanted to play. He tossed the ball up and down in his hand, unsure what to do. Just then, his mother opened the back door and called him.

"Christopher! Can you please take Marbles for a walk before dinner?" Marbles burst out the back door and ran to Christopher, wagging his tail and dragging his leash behind him.

"Sure, Mom," Christopher called back.

He pocketed the orange ball then picked up his dog's leash and started the long struggle down the driveway. He really didn't want to get dragged around by Marbles. Tonight, right now, he wanted to be brave. He wanted to get to the bottom of whatever was going on in that park.

"Come on boy, we're going this way," Christopher grunted as he used all his strength to drag Marbles toward the park gates. The neighbourhood was quiet. There were no cars driving by, no streetcars, and very few people were out on the streets. The old man with the thick glasses, hat, and the brown coat wasn't sitting on the bench down the sidewalk. Christopher attached Marbles' leash to the gates and drew up all his courage. He was going back in.

"I have to find out what's going on in there, Marbles. Just stay here, bark if anyone comes." Marbles whined and licked his lips, quivering on the sidewalk. Christopher contorted himself once again and just barely managed to squeeze through the bars.

He stepped into the park and looked around. Again, it was very silent, more silent than it should have been. Except for the bubbling of the seahorse fountain, it was like he was in the middle of the countryside. There was the little apple tree, almost bare of leaves, but still bearing delicious-looking fruit. Two benches surrounded the tree. The bushes around the outside of the park were still.

Christopher took a deep breath. He was determined to be courageous. "Hello?" he whispered, but it came out as a croak. So he tried again, a little louder this time. "Hello!" he squeaked, but at least audibly. His heart was hammering in his chest.

The park was still and quiet.

"Uh, thank you for returning my orange ball," he said, a little braver this time. Suddenly he felt really foolish, like a little kid imagining things, talking to an empty park like a crazy person.

The ball could have bounced off something and rolled back out on its own, couldn't it?

Then he heard it. The wind rattling the barren dry leaves, or maybe it was something else. A gravelly voice said, "Megathon dret alba." But Christopher also heard it say, "He left the monster outside."

Christopher gasped but tried not to scream. He bit his tongue and tried to remember to breathe. He managed to stutter out, "Uhhh, heelllo? I know you're here. You threw apples at me, but you tried not to hit me. You clapped at my guitar music. You returned my ball." His teeth were actually chattering together, he was so scared. But he was also determined.

"Morten gella dorth!" came another gravelly voice, but sweeter, which translated into, "You're frightening him!"

Christopher's eyes were like giant saucers now. Clearly there were two voices, two *somethings*, in the bushes.

But *what?*

He didn't get to find out what. At that moment Marbles stopped whining. A tall figure was standing at the gates. A really, really tall lady.

She was standing on the sidewalk patting his dog's head (who, unlike any *good* watchdog, was sniffing her hand and wagging his tail) and peering into the park.

She called into the park, "Hello? Boy? Are you in there?"

Christopher wasn't sure whether he should answer her or dive into the bushes and hide.

It wasn't an easy choice. Christopher really wanted to hide, very badly, but since the bushes had strange voices in them, he decided they might not make such an entirely great hiding spot. He hesitated, but in the end had little choice but to answer the lady.

"Yuh ... yes. I'm here. I think you mean me? I think I'm who you mean?" Christopher jibbered. He stepped away from the tree and walked toward the gate. The tall lady smiled nicely at him through the fence and pointed toward a small handle inside the gate.

"Pull that handle there, would you please?"

Christopher hadn't noticed it, but there was the outline of a small doorway cut into the gate, next to the gatepost. It was kind of a secret, hidden door, which you probably wouldn't see unless someone pointed it out to you. He pulled on the handle, and the door swung inward with a creak.

The tall lady undid Marble's leash and stooped to walk through the door with him. The dog was very happy to be on the same side of the fence as his master and licked Christopher excitedly. The lady handed Christopher the leash. Then she added, "You'd better hold on to him tightly."

"Thank you," Christopher said. "Uh, I'll see you then."

He was starting to go through the doorway, back out to the street, when he heard the whispery, growly voice again. It sounded very close to him, and Christopher heard it say very clearly, practically in his ear, "Megathon alta!" At the same time he also heard it say, "Get that monster out of here."

Many things happened next, rather quickly. At the very instant in which the voice spoke, Marbles caught the scent of something. He snapped his head up, sniffed twice, then dove into the bushes, yanking Christopher off his feet. Christopher landed with a thud and dropped the leash. The tall lady rushed to grab the leash, but Marbles was off and running madly through the bushes, barking and chasing something frantically.

For a moment, the bushes were alive with squeals and grunts and shrieks. Christopher and the lady rushed around, trying to grab Marbles, who was just as madly chasing and running away from them. The dog, the boy, the lady, and the *somethings* in the bushes dashed the circuit of the park twice, before Christopher somehow managed to make a giant leap and land on Marbles' back. Boy and dog both landed with a grunt on the ground, Christopher on top. He grabbed the leash, panting as he lay on his dog.

"Sorry. Are you okay?" Christopher managed to say.

The tall lady had taken a seat on one of the park benches. She was mopping her brow. "My, your dog is quite … athletic," she croaked, trying to catch her breath.

Marbles was whining and wriggling and champing his teeth, staring up into the apple tree. There was a rustling above them, but Christopher couldn't look up into the tree AND keep a tight hold on his dog at the same time. He was barely big enough to weigh Marbles down as it was. If he moved a muscle, then the dog would be off and running again.

"I'm Cassandra Daye, D-A-Y-E, by the way. That's my store across the street," the tall lady said, still trying to catch her breath.

"Oh. I see. Candles by Daye, with an 'e'. I get it." Christopher was doing his best to be polite, which wasn't all that easy under the circumstances. "I'm Christopher Canning. I live next door," he managed to say. He could feel Marbles tensing beneath him, readying himself for a monstrous leap up the trunk of the apple tree.

"Hello, Christopher." She seemed uneasy, like people do when they're hiding something.

She kept darting little glances up into the apple tree, then back down at him. She cleared her throat, about to speak, when a gentle, whispery voice said, "Blethem morgount." Christopher heard it say, "He seems nice." It came from the top of the apple tree.

Christopher tensed as Marbles went rigid beneath him, ready to spring. "Okay, what was that voice? Who seems nice?" Christopher asked.

"Voice? What voice? Oh, that? Wind in the leaves, don't you think? Do you like this park? It's very old … the city is thinking of removing it, building apartments. It's not much use for most people … the fountain watered horses a long time ago … it's still quite lovely…"

Christopher knew she was trying to distract him. His mother did that, talked too much about things that weren't relevant whenever she was nervous or trying to draw his attention elsewhere. It worked when he was little, sometimes.

The deeper, growlier voice said, "Megathon mebahtu." Christopher heard it say, "The monster smells bad."

Christopher's eyes grew wide as he looked up into Cassandra's face. "Did ... did you hear that?" he whispered. "What is it?"

Cassandra Daye bit her lip. "Oh, I really don't think I should ... nothing ..."

Christopher couldn't help it. He lost his patience, and with his last breath, he yelled out, "PLEASE TELL ME WHAT IS TALKING TO ME IN THE TREE!"

"Oh well, I'm not sure ..."

And that's when Christopher Canning's arms gave out, and Marbles-the-monster made a mighty leap into the air, loudly snapping his teeth together ...

... just missing a gargoyle as it flew out of the apple tree and lurched off into the night sky.

Marbles leapt into the air like an Olympic vault champion (Cassandra was right, he really WAS athletic) and snapped his jaws at the gargoyle, but the dog missed the creature by a hair.

The gargoyle escaped.

Christopher stared as the gargoyle careened into the sky. It looked like a fat black bat or maybe a giant frightened June bug, but it wasn't as graceful. The gargoyle really wasn't very good at flying. It barely got out of the way of Marbles' jaws and didn't have very good control of where it was going. It banged into a tree and almost crashed into a lamppost in its hurry to get away.

But the gargoyle made it across the street and settled on the roof of Candles by Daye. Christopher stood with his mouth open, staring. Marbles was barking furiously at the gate. The gargoyle was outlined against the roof of Cassandra's store for a moment, and Christopher could make out its head over the edge of the rooftop. The gargoyle shook its wings like an angry goose, looked straight at Christopher, then stuck its tongue out at him.

"How RUDE!" he gasped.

He wheeled around to look at Cassandra, who was busily examining her nails. Marbles flopped down onto the park grass and panted, tired out from all the excitement.

"Was that ... a *gargoyle?*" Christopher whispered.

Cassandra looked up from her nail-examination and smiled politely. "Was *what* a gargoyle?"

Christopher was astonished. He wasn't sure what to say next, but he decided a direct question might be best. "Did I just see a *gargoyle* fly across the street and land on the roof of your store?"

Cassandra nodded slowly but wouldn't look him in the eye. Her nails seemed much more interesting to her.

"Did I hear it *talking* to me?" he asked.

She nodded, a little faster this time. "You're lucky you can understand them. I can't. Only children and some lucky adults understand them properly ..." she said wistfully. Christopher suddenly felt a little sorry for Cassandra, since she sounded so sad — but he needed answers, VERY CLEAR and VERY SIMPLE answers. He pressed on.

"So ... just to be clear, there is a gargoyle ... *living* in this park?" He realized he didn't sound very intelligent, but he didn't care.

Cassandra looked him in the eye this time and nodded. "Well, *two* gargoyles actually."

At that very moment another gargoyle flew past Christopher, but this one could fly a little better and didn't bang into anything. It was so quiet and stealthy that Marbles didn't even notice it. Christopher watched as it flew across the street and joined the first gargoyle on the roof of Candles by Daye, disappearing around an old chimney.

"Am I losing my marbles?" he asked and flopped down on the bench beside Cassandra. At the sound of his name, the dog raised his head and barked.

"Not you. I know I haven't lost you, you crazy dog. I mean me, *my* marbles. Am I going crazy?"

"No, Christopher, you're not crazy," Cassandra said slowly. Christopher looked at her closely. She seemed like a nice, normal lady, if really tall. She didn't seem crazy, or like a liar. But she didn't want to tell him the truth, either. She was very reluctant to say anything at all.

But before he could ask anything else, the back door of his house creaked open, casting a circle of warm yellow light to the edge of the park. His mother called his name.

"I'm coming, Mom!" Christopher shouted back. "It's dinner time. I have to go!" Marbles jumped up and shook himself. Cassandra and Christopher walked to the hidden doorway and back out to the sidewalk. Cassandra practically had to crawl on her hands and knees to fit through. The doorway swung closed with a click, and when it was shut, Christopher almost couldn't see it. You'd only see it if you knew where to look.

Cassandra said, "Come by my store tomorrow after school. I'll make you tea. We'll talk. Oh, and for now, maybe don't tell anyone about the gargoyles. Bye, Christopher," she said thoughtfully, then crossed the street, which was empty and quiet.

Christopher turned to go to his house but noticed there were two gargoyles on the park gateposts.

"Cassandra, what about these two?" Christopher called across the street after her.

"Stone! Just gargoyle statues with water-spouts. I remove them when the real gargoyles want to sit there," she said, then she vanished into her store with a little tinkle of the bell.

Christopher didn't say a word at dinner. He was too busy mulling over the facts.

Fact number one: there were two gargoyles *living* in the park next door to his house.

Fact number two: it was likely going to be *quite* interesting.

Chapter Twelve
The English Garden: Arabella

James was lying on the grass, looking up into the autumn sky. The days were already shorter, the nights just a little cooler than they had been, and he was going home, back to Toronto in a few days time. His summer visit with his grandfather was coming to an end.

He listened to bees still busy in the flowers and the sound of the fountain in the pond, spouting water onto the dark lily pads and lurking frogs. He was going to miss the place. It was nothing like his busy life back in Toronto.

He knew he was going to miss his grandfather, too, even with his odd wardrobe and his obsession with statues.

They had spent all summer scanning newspapers and books from all over the globe, from Italy and England, Canada and Japan, searching for "what's lost." It seemed like an impossible task, especially since his grandfather wasn't all that entirely clear about WHAT was lost, exactly.

James heard a noise and sat up.

WHIZZ! He ducked just in time: an apple shot right past his head and crashed into the garden seat, spraying shattered apple pieces all over him.

"Hey! Cut it out, whoever you are!" He scrambled on all fours across the grass, and dove for cover behind a half-finished statue of flowers. Apple after apple smashed into the statue above his head. He peeked out and caught a glimpse of a leathery arm and a horned head.

"Arabella! I'm leaving soon, don't you want to make friends with me before I go?"

The apples stopped. A sweet, whispery gargoyle voice called back, "Mashrad bellatro!" but James heard it say, "Defend yourself, boy!"

James gulped. He knew what was coming. Still hiding, he scooped all the apples he could, lobbing them back in the direction of the thrower in the trees. The garden rang with the sound of apples, apples everywhere! The apple war raged until James thought his arms would give out.

But finally the apples stopped coming (there weren't any more in easy reach). He heard a strange, raspy sound then, which took him a moment to understand: the gargoyle Arabella was *laughing*!

Have you ever heard a gargoyle laugh? Imagine a sound something between a small, barking dog and a rattling bag of bones. James lay exhausted among the apples listening to laughing Arabella, and found that he was laughing, too.

They might be naughty. They could be surprising. They might bury you in leaves, drench you with water, and wing apples at you when you weren't looking.

But James was NOT expecting that a gargoyle could make you *laugh*.

Chapter Thirteen
Candles by Daye, in the Afternoon

The next day at school, Christopher avoided Katherine. He didn't know if she knew he'd been in the park again, and he really didn't want to find out. He did his best to stay out of her sight.

After school though, it was obvious he wasn't going to be able to avoid Katherine any longer. He was late leaving his classroom and when he got to the streetcar stop, Katherine was standing there.

He didn't have any choice, he had to wait with her.

"Hi," he mumbled.

She looked at him, and looked away. "Hi," she said quietly.

They waited in total silence. Katherine read a book, ignoring him. Christopher looked at the sky. Looked at his shoes. Was very interested in the dirt under his fingernail. Stared straight ahead. And sighed with relief when the streetcar finally came.

Katherine went to the back of the streetcar. Christopher sat right behind the driver, as far from her as he could.

He could see a problem arising.

Cassandra had invited him for tea this afternoon after school. Last night, she'd very clearly said, "Come by my store tomorrow after school for tea." He didn't want to disappoint her if she was waiting for him. He didn't want to appear rude, and he DID want to know more about the gargoyles. He'd been thinking about them all day. He couldn't STOP thinking about them. The whole class had laughed their heads off when the teacher asked him a question in math class and he answered, "Gargoyle." He wasn't paying attention, and when he opened his mouth to answer, that's what popped out. Luckily, Katherine wasn't in class at that moment.

He was invited to Candles by Daye for tea, and he wanted to go. But Katherine was obviously visiting Cassandra's store today, too. They would both be there …

… and he was pretty sure Katherine would disapprove.

He bit his lip and glanced down the streetcar, which was empty except for the two of them. Katherine was busy reading.

His heart was pounding when he got off the streetcar. He let Katherine go first, and she zipped ahead of him along the sidewalk, then darted through the green door of Candles by Daye. Christopher heard the doorbell tinkle, caught the scent of cinnamon, then watched the door slam behind her.

What was he going to do?

He stood for a while on the sidewalk in front of the store, fiddling with his backpack strap and scratching the top of his foot against his calf. He pushed his glasses up his nose. He glanced across the street at his house, but no one was home. Claire came home and walked the dog at lunch every day now, so Marbles was taken care of, at least for the moment.

Christopher took a deep breath, reached for the door handle … then heard a crash inside the store. Suddenly someone was shouting.

"You're the thief!" someone yelled. "Now get out!" The door burst open and a man with thick glasses, a white straw hat, and a large brown coat barrelled onto the sidewalk, banged into Christopher and stormed off down the street muttering. He seemed very angry.

Christopher was astonished.

"Come in, Christopher!" Cassandra said pleasantly from the doorway. She was quite calm for someone who was just yelling at a customer.

"Who … who was *that?*" Christopher croaked.

"Don't worry about him, he's just a nasty person who drops by from time to time. Tea?"

She seemed so nice that Christopher could only smile and nod. He really couldn't believe such angry words had come out of this pleasant, calm lady. Maybe yelling at the customers was just another thing that he'd have to get used to about Toronto? As Cassandra poured the tea, Christopher looked around.

It was a strange store, filled with statues, incense, candles, and books about yoga. There were healing chime balls (whatever those were) and strings of beads and crystals hanging from the ceiling, along with dream catchers, bandanas, and Toronto tourist postcards. It was like an antique store, but with more stuff in it. He could tell it was really, really old.

He reached forward to take a sip of tea ... and froze.

Someone was coming down the stairs at the back of the store. The stairs must have gone up to the roof, because a few September leaves blew down into the store with the walker.

It was Katherine.

Chapter Fourteen
The Stone Lion Stands

It was James's last day in England, and his grandfather had woken that morning determined to go on a road trip. James was delighted! He hadn't seen much of England at all since he'd been there, nothing really except London on the day he landed and his grandfather's beautiful old garden and thatched cottage ever since. He wanted to see at least some of the country before leaving for home.

He was excited at the thought of going for a drive through the countryside, but grew a little worried. He hadn't seen a car anywhere on his grandfather's property, and he hoped they weren't travelling across the countryside by balloon, or penny-farthing bicycle or something (with his grampa, you just never knew). James followed his grandfather into an old shed and gasped when the old man pulled a huge sheet off an antique 1920s road car. Thick dust filled the shed and made James cough and rub his eyes.

"Grampa Gregory! Is THAT your car? We're going for a drive in THAT?" But his grandfather didn't answer him. Instead he opened the trunk and pulled out a box, which looked just as dusty as the sheet. It creaked open, and James tried not to look too worried at what he saw inside: *two* leather caps and *two* pairs of giant goggles. His grandfather took one leather cap out of the box, blew thick dust off it, and handed it to James. Then he picked up the other cap and started fiddling with the leather strap under his chin.

James recognized these caps: they were the kind of caps that flying aces wore in their bi-planes in the First World War. So today his grandfather was going to look like a flying ace?

James gingerly lifted the leather cap to his head but heaved a silent sigh of relief when it didn't fit. It was much too big. He looked up at his grandfather and nearly jumped out of his skin. His grandfather was wearing his leather cap and the giant goggles, which made his eyes look enormous.

"Okay, no hat, but you'll need the goggles," his grandfather said, passing them to him. Unfortunately, the goggles fit, and James had no choice but to wear them as he and his grandfather pulled slowly out of the cottage driveway then cruised through the English countryside. His grandfather drove the old-fashioned car with big headlights and leather seats and footrails along roads beside fields of ripe wheat and barley.

They passed cows and sheep dotting the slopes and valleys of the rolling green English hills. There were beautiful farmhouses and tractors travelling along slowly, hauling huge mounds of fresh hay. Occasionally they passed through a small town, with giggling children and adults waving at their antique car. James's grandfather always beeped the horn, which made a loud, deep honk, drawing more shrieks and giggles and waves from the people of the town.

James's grandfather was right: he DID need the goggles. The old car barely had a windshield, and by the time they drove through a tiny country village and parked on the main street, the goggles were covered with bugs. And not all of them were dead.

His grandfather pulled a picnic basket out of the trunk and led James to the edge of the town, to an old abandoned church. The churchyard gate creaked open very loudly, and as James stepped into the church courtyard, he gasped.

It was the most beautiful place he'd ever seen. The church walls were golden, still warm in the afternoon sun. A little stream ran along beside the church and an ancient, overgrown apple orchard looked as though it hadn't been tended in years. In the distance, green hills and chestnut trees rolled away as far as he could see.

He breathed deep. It was quiet except for the bubbling of the little stream, and the air was sweet with the scent of the tiny, wild apples.

But what drew James's attention most was a statue sitting all alone on a pedestal in the middle of the courtyard. It was made of stone, and it must have been hundreds of years old.

It was a lion, regal and proud, facing west. James moved over to the statue and ran his hand along its golden stone back, which was warm and glowing in the afternoon sun. His hand hovered over the lion's left ear, which was broken off. James realized something was underfoot: he was standing on a piece of stone, which he picked up and rolled in his hand. He slowly fit the piece of broken stone back onto the lion's ear. It fit perfectly; the left ear was whole again.

"Do you come to life and roar at night?" James whispered in the lion's ear. It stared into the distance with fierce stone eyes. James felt a strange kinship with the lion and lingered a long time, looking into the distance with it, listening to the bubbling stream nearby. It made him wonder who else had lived there? What had the lion seen in its long, long life in this tiny, tucked-away place?

Who had broken its left ear?

Finally he joined his grandfather beside the apple orchard. "I love this place," he said as the old man was laying out a picnic lunch on the grass beside the stream.

His grandfather chuckled. "It's a special place for me, too," he said.

The pair sat on the autumn grass with the smell of apples heavy all around them. They ate sandwiches and drank warm mint tea from a flask. And they talked.

"This churchyard is over four hundred years old, and it's seen a lot of history, James. That empty field right over there is filled with the remains of hundreds of villagers who died of the plague in 1665," Grampa Gregory said, waving his hand casually over his shoulder. James looked but saw only sun shining on waving green grass. England was a mysterious and very old place indeed.

Suddenly, something landed in the grass at James's feet. He brushed bread crumbs off his hands and stood up. An apple core was lying in the grass. James shaded his eyes and looked up into the church high above him.

"Who's up there?" he called, but his grandfather whispered at him to be quiet.

"Look carefully, James. We have a visitor," he said quietly. James screwed up his eyes and peered as hard as he could. He could just make out a tiny horned head and wings at the top of the church parapet, hiding in the ivy.

"Arabella? Is that Arabella up there, Grampa?" James whispered.

"Yes. She loves it here, too. She flies here at night and often stays for days. I was a little boy and sitting right here the first time I met Theodorus, Septimus, and Arabella. They threw apples at me then, too." Grampa Gregory smiled as he remembered that long-ago day.

Another apple landed at James's feet.

"Don't worry, James, she doesn't want an apple war, not today. She's just saying hello."

James craned his head back and looked up to the top of the church, straining to see the little gargoyle again, but she was too well hidden. A trill of gargoyle laughter floated down to him.

It was strange, but suddenly he could imagine another boy, in another time, doing exactly what he was doing: staring up into the ivy, listening to a whispery, haunting, gargoyle laugh, and wondering how to make friends.

Chapter Fifteen
The Watching Man

Katherine put her hands on her hips. "Christopher, what are you doing here?" she demanded. She didn't seem very happy. Christopher tried not to look worried.

Cassandra came to his rescue. "I invited him, Katherine. He was in the park last night and met the gargoyles by accident. I invited him to come today for tea."

Katherine walked over to Christopher. She stood before him and looked him steadily in the eye, crossing her arms. He tried not to flinch.

"Well, Christopher Canning, it seems we have no choice but to be friends. How are you with keeping secrets?" she asked.

Christopher thought about all the times his older brothers had kept secrets from him (but never his sister, who didn't care much for secrets). He was never allowed in on any of them. It would be a pleasure to have a secret of his own, a big one, which he wouldn't share. It would be just his.

"Okay, I guess. I don't usually have anything to keep secret."

Katherine looked at him a long while and finally said, "Come up to the roof." Christopher followed her up the small staircase to the top of the store. She pushed open a squeaky door, and the two of them stepped out onto the rooftop.

Christopher thought the view from his bedroom window was good, but this view was incredible. The city was bright and sparkling off to the west, the huge towers glinting in the afternoon sun. The shining lake at the foot of the city was a bright green pool, disappearing into the distance as far as he could see. The CN Tower was like a huge sentinel, standing watch over everything.

On the rooftop there were tiny trees in buckets, apple trees like the one across the street in the park, bearing ripe fruit. There was a rain barrel brimming with fresh rainwater, a tin cup attached to the side. Pillows and blankets and comfortable chairs waited in a circle under an awning, so you could sit and talk there any time, rain or shine. There was a propane heater to warm up the space.

A small garden gnome statue stood off by itself in a corner against the chimney. It looked badly battered, and Christopher noticed apples smashed at its feet and on the wall behind it. Someone was a good shot.

The rooftop was a friendly place. Katherine sat in one of the comfortable wooden chairs and pulled a blanket over herself. She beckoned Christopher to a chair beside her.

"Sit," she said.

He perched on a lawn chair, but he couldn't relax. He really just wanted to run away.

"It's okay, Christopher. I don't bite," she smiled then added, "The gargoyles might, though, you should probably watch out for that."

"Uh, yeah, okay," he stammered. The thought of explaining to his mother that he had a gargoyle bite made his head swim. He had the sudden horrible desire to giggle madly. Instead, he forced himself to say something. "What do you call the gargoyles?"

"Their names are Gargoth and Ambergine."

"Have they always lived in the park across the street?"

"Oh, no! They're over four hundred years old, they've lived a lot of places. They want to live here in Toronto now, near Cassandra and me. The park is perfect for them … but I don't think they can stay." She paused, suddenly quiet.

"Why not?"

She sighed. "They have an enemy, Christopher. An obsessed old man who wants to steal them and lock them away … he's done it before. He locked Gargoth up for seventy years."

"An enemy? Locked him up?"

"Yes. He's called the Collector. He's sitting right over there," Katherine said nonchalantly. She waved over her shoulder in the direction of the library, a few rooftops away.

It was getting dark, but Christopher squinted and could make out a figure sitting on the library rooftop garden bench. It was an old man wearing thick glasses, a hat, and a heavy brown coat. And he was staring straight at them.

Christopher found it creepy. Slowly he realized that he recognized the man. "I ... I've seen him before. He sits outside the park in the mornings sometimes, on that bench down the sidewalk, and I think he was in the store this afternoon. Cassandra yelled at him," he whispered.

"That's him. And most nights he sits over there on that rooftop staring at us, until the library closes."

"Aren't you afraid of him?" Christopher asked a little nervously, trying not to glance over at the silent figure.

Katherine shook her head. "No. He just makes me mad, actually. All he wants are the gargoyles, and he can't get them."

"But why not? I mean, he could grab them any time, couldn't he? What's to stop him?"

"They aren't helpless, you know. For one thing, they can fly. For another, they have each other. Plus, they have us to help them. Cassandra and I keep watch over them in the park, and they can always come up here to the store rooftop. They're pretty safe up here. They used to stay in my backyard at home, too, but the Collector knows where I live now, so it isn't safe anymore. Other than me, Cassandra and my parents, no one else knows about them. Oh, and now you."

Christopher was awestruck. He couldn't believe that he knew something so important, and so secret. Suddenly he had a million questions about the gargoyles, which Katherine answered very patiently (and if you've been following their story, you already know most of the answers). He wanted to know all about them, what they ate, drank, where they came from.

Christopher's last question took Katherine by surprise: "Why are the gargoyles alive?"

She shook her head. "No one knows. We _do_ know that the man who created them was a mysterious French stonemason named Tallus. Gargoth and Ambergine both have his stonemason's mark, on their backs between their wings." Katherine dug a pencil and a piece of paper out of her backpack and quickly drew an image, which she showed to Christopher. It looked like this:

"His stonemason's mark was a circle with two diamonds inside. If we could find out more about Tallus, we might be able to discover more about the gargoyles, but there's no trace of the Tallus family anymore."

Then Katherine told Christopher the long story of the gargoyles' lives, together and apart. She went right back to the beginning, to the English churchyard in 1604 where Gargoth was created, then to France where he met Ambergine in 1665, then to Paris in 1778, then to New York City in 1860. Christopher sat listening to the gargoyles' story, entranced.

Afternoon turned to evening as Katherine talked and Christopher listened. Cassandra came up to the rooftop and had Christopher phone home and ask if he could stay for dinner, which was lentil stew (something he'd never had before and wasn't entirely sure he ever wanted again). After dinner, Cassandra switched on the portable propane heater, and the rooftop turned into a cozy place.

Cassandra brought armloads of mismatched candles up from the store. Her store was Candles by Daye, after all, and they sat among the glowing candlelight, Katherine telling a long story, and Christopher listening and occasionally darting uneasy glances over at the library rooftop.

It would have been perfect, except for the dark figure sitting there, watching them, still as a statue the entire time.

Chapter Sixteen
Welcome to the Rooftop

It was getting late. Christopher shot another nervous look at the library rooftop, but the old man was gone. The library was closed for the evening, and somehow listening to the gargoyles' story, he hadn't noticed the old man get up and leave the rooftop.

BANG! A loud thump made Christopher jump. A gargoyle had landed on the roof and smacked into a lawn chair, which fell over. Another gargoyle landed quietly behind him, a sweeter-looking one, gentler and smaller. Christopher was surprised how similar they were, with the same leathery skin, the same wings, the same pouches at their side. Now that he could see them up close, he could easily tell which was Gargoth and which was Ambergine. The girl gargoyle was somehow more girlish, a little more pretty (if you could ever call a gargoyle pretty).

Ambergine waddled up to Christopher and put out her claw. Christopher hesitated then shook it.

"Snarthen freema olat," the gargoyle said in her breezy, whispery voice, but Christopher heard her say, "Did you get your orange ball?"

Gargoth stomped to the apple basket and started lobbing apples carelessly at the gnome statue. He was an amazing shot, and the poor gnome didn't stand a chance. It was rocking back and forth on its pedestal in grave danger of being smashed to bits.

Christopher turned back to Ambergine. "Yes, I got my ball back, thank you. My brothers and I use it for ball-hockey but it actually belongs to my dog. Sorry if he scared you last night. You must be Ambergine, nice to meet you," Christopher said, still carefully shaking the gargoyle's claw. It was cool and leathery, and looked VERY SHARP.

Then Gargoth spoke in his growly, raspy voice, like winter leaves shaking in the breeze. He spoke in gargoyle, and this is what he said: "Margo beshu vaunt." Christopher heard him say, "The Collector was watching."

Then Gargoth picked up an apple and threw it so hard at the gnome that the top of its peaked cap broke into pieces. Christopher jumped, but the others didn't seem to notice.

Katherine scowled. "Why won't he just go away?"

"He's not going away, you know that, Katherine, not until he gets what he wants," Ambergine said quietly in gargoyle. Gargoth came and joined them, sitting on a cushion at Katherine's feet. The candles were getting low, and it was so late that the city had fallen quiet all around them. Christopher realized he was tired and cold.

"I … I guess I should go. Thanks for telling me the gargoyles' story. It was nice to meet you," he said to the gargoyles, but Gargoth just scowled and turned his back. Christopher thought he heard him mutter "blethem" and "imbecile" at the same time, but he couldn't be entirely sure.

Ambergine, on the other hand, hopped down from Katherine's lap and waddled up to Christopher. She beckoned to him to bend down, which he did.

She whispered in his ear in gargoyle, "I'm glad you've come, Christopher Canning. Katherine is going to need your help, I know it. We all will."

It was time to go. Cassandra and Katherine walked Christopher to the door, and Cassandra said, "You should come again tomorrow. Katherine will be here."

He said thank-you and crossed the street to his house. He was burning to know more about the gargoyles and couldn't wait to go back to the store. More importantly, though, he noticed that Katherine smiled at him, just a little, when she said goodbye.

Chapter Seventeen
The English Garden: Goodbyes

James stood beside his packed suitcase. He was wearing his travelling clothes, and he was waiting. He'd been waiting for some time. He looked anxiously at his watch. If his grandfather didn't hurry up, he was going to miss his flight back to Canada. He had enjoyed his summer in England, but it was time to go home to Toronto. School had already started.

He looked into the beautiful autumn sky, azure and golden and white with clouds. He cast his eyes over the pretty thatched cottage and quiet grounds. The garden was in its full, last days of glory, with asters and late-blooming flowers. The apple trees were literally groaning with heavy fruit. He heard a noise behind him and turned.

The three gargoyles were standing on the gravel driveway before him.

The first was squat and very weathered and ancient-looking, wearing a naughty grin: Septimus.

The second was large and heavy and had a gigantic ram's head framed by curly horns: Theodorus.

The third was the smallest and daintiest, with tiny horns and leathery arms folded across her chest: Arabella.

All three had wings, and each wore a pouch at their side bulging with intriguing shapes. James hadn't seen them all together at once. Now they were standing before him, he could see they were each very different.

But there was a sameness there, too.

They seemed shy and reluctant to speak.

James's grandfather walked up to them, dressed in a black leather jacket with huge leather gloves, his First World War flying ace leather cap, and the giant, bug-like goggles (for the bugs).

"Ready to go then, Grampa?" James asked, since none of the creatures nor the old man seemed inclined to speak. He hated goodbyes, and there was a plane to catch.

"I think Septimus, Theodorus, and Arabella would like to say something to you first," his grandfather answered. His eyes looked enormous behind the goggles.

The old man glared sternly at the gargoyles, who reminded James for all the world of a troop of actors gone slightly wrong. There was much sighing and rolling of eyes, crossing of arms, and scowling, until finally Theodorus spoke.

"Wegoth merry fleg," he said in his deep, booming voice. James heard him say, "You've been interesting."

The boy wasn't entirely sure if this was a compliment, but he inclined his head and politely said, "Thank you, Theodorus. So have you."

The ancient and weathered gargoyle stepped forward then, and muttered, "Blegem thents brog." But James heard this gargoyle say, "Sorry about interrupting your reading all summer."

Again, James very respectfully inclined his head and answered the creature: "Thank you, Septimus. I managed to get my reading done, despite your … piles of leaves."

Finally, the smallest of the three gargoyles spoke. She said impatiently, "Gorgen ballia treshie. Alia morim." Which James heard as, "You're still a terrible shot. You've been a great target, though."

Grampa Gregory said, "Arabella," very sternly, and turned his bushy eyebrows and hugely magnified eyes down upon the gargoyle, who fidgeted.

She dropped her head and said very softly, "Beffi morgaunt," which James heard as, "And I shall miss you."

There were a few moments of surprised silence, since this gargoyle had barely spoken to James all summer and had only engaged him by pelting apples at him. He'd wondered about this. It had taken a while for them to warm up to him, but eventually the other two gargoyles spoke to him now and then. Septimus even sat and smoked a pipe around him in the evenings, and spoke occasionally of history and past friends and adventures (most of which centred around people named Elizabeth and Napoleon). But this little gargoyle hadn't sought him out all summer. She seemed more thoroughly alone and somehow sadder than the other two.

For the third time James bowed his head and again said graciously, "Thank you, Arabella. I'll miss you too. I'll miss all of you."

There was a long, awkward silence between all five, the old man, boy, and three creatures, until Theodorus suddenly stepped forward and crunched across the driveway on his heavy, taloned feet. He pulled something out of his pouch, which he dropped into James's hand. It was a small stone carving of a gargoyle, with wings, a leathery head, and a pouch at its side. It looked similar to the gargoyles before him, but not exactly like any of them. It had its own look.

The boy studied the little gargoyle statue for a moment, amazed at how intricate it was. It was made from soft, greyish stone and was carefully tooled, with a naughty face, wings, and a tiny pouch at its side. James had seen Theodorus carving a small piece of stone all summer, but had no idea until just now what he'd been creating.

He was touched at the gargoyle's gift.

He looked up to say, "Thank you, Theodorus," but there was no point. The gargoyles had all vanished back into the apple trees and the surrounding garden. He placed the little stone gargoyle carving into his pocket and carefully patted it.

"Never mind, James. It's a great honour to get a gift from a gargoyle." Grampa Gregory placed his gloved hand on his grandson's shoulder and passed him a heavy leather bag with the initials "G.T." on it in gold lettering next to some golden symbols.

"I have a gift for you, too," his grandfather said.

James took the bag and almost dropped it, it was so heavy. It was the size of his hockey bag at home, but three times heavier.

"Thanks, Grampa. What is it?"

"Open it, boy!"

James gingerly peeked into the old, musty leather bag, and blinked. It was filled with tools, old, old tools. They looked like ... hammers and chisels and sharp saws of different sizes and shapes. There was a three-sided file that looked like something a prisoner would use to break out of prison. There was a chisel, or maybe it was an awl (a term he'd learned from his reading in *The History of Stonemasons in Europe*), which looked wickedly sharp.

James looked up politely at his grandfather for some explanation.

"Stonemason's tools! They were mine when I was your age! You never know when you'll need the right tool for stonemasonry!"

His grandfather seemed very proud of his gift, his enormously heavy gift, so James could only say, "Great, Grampa, thank you. I'm sure these will be ... handy."

His grandfather beamed then strode across the gravel driveway, jumped into the 1920s road car and revved up the engine (with much black smoke belching out the back). James strapped on his own goggles. Much as he hated them, he didn't want to be picking bugs out of his teeth on the plane all the way home across the Atlantic Ocean.

"Come on! Let's go!" the old man shouted.

James picked up his modest suitcase and hoisted the heavy bag of stonemason's tools, then took one last look at the pretty thatched cottage and the English garden with his grandfather's half-finished statues and soothing fountains. He knew the gargoyles were probably peeking out of the trees at him (perhaps with an apple at the ready), and he made a promise to himself: he WOULD come back next summer, and he WOULD continue to look through newspapers and report to his grandfather anything he found out about statues ... and gargoyles.

Although in Toronto, that really didn't seem very likely.

Chapter Eighteen
The Stone Replicas

A few weeks had passed since Christopher and Katherine talked on the rooftop. Since that night, Christopher had visited Cassandra's store almost every day after school, doing his homework with Katherine and talking about the gargoyles. Cassandra usually sat knitting and listening, or tended to a customer. Once in a while the gargoyles would join them inside, but usually they were across the street in the park, or up on the rooftop. They preferred the outdoors.

After that first night, Christopher didn't notice the Collector sitting on the park bench outside the gates, and he hadn't been in the store again. He *was* still there watching from the library rooftop at night, though. Christopher tried not to think too much about him. He was there, but since neither Katherine nor Cassandra paid him much attention, Christopher tried not to, either.

There were a few chores for Katherine and Christopher. Apple cores had to be removed from the rooftop, and from the park. Smashed garden gnome pieces had to be swept up. Cassandra had a steady supply of gnomes from one of her vendors, so there was always a fresh one to be carted up to the rooftop.

And someone had to tend the stone statues at the park gates every day. They had to be removed whenever the real gargoyles wanted to sit there and look over the street. The statues had to be placed back on the gateposts whenever the real gargoyles grew bored and left their perches.

It was a bit tricky, since the statues were heavy, and it had to be done without anyone noticing, which wasn't exactly all that easy on a busy downtown street. Cassandra kept the gargoyle statues hidden in a yellow canvas backpack under the counter in her store. She had bought them years before in a garage sale (she had always loved gargoyles). Christopher or Katherine would stagger across the road with the heavy canvas backpack, sometimes three or four times a day, until Katherine put her foot down and said it could only be twice a day, no more.

The statues didn't really look much like Gargoth and Ambergine, either, but Christopher seemed to be the only person to notice. They didn't have pouches, for one thing, and they were identical, for another. He wondered how no one passing by on the street could notice that sometimes the gargoyles at the gates were wet and steaming in the rain, but at other times they were spouting rain water.

Gargoth and Ambergine didn't spout rain water; the stone gargoyles did.

Gargoth and Ambergine steamed gently when it rained; the cold stone gargoyles did not.

Christopher also noticed that Gargoth hated the statues and refused to go anywhere near them. He even used them for target practice and thought nothing of pelting them with apples. When Christopher asked Katherine about it, she said, "If you'd seen yourself doing a million weird things as a statue, you'd hate them too." It was puzzling, but it was the only answer Christopher got.

Placing the statues on the gates was risky and took a quick, sneaky switch. Christopher didn't know it, but his sister Claire was beginning to notice that he was awfully interested in the gargoyles at the gate, and in the little park. One day she hid behind the living room curtains of the house and watched with interest as he switched the stone gargoyles. She couldn't see exactly what he was doing, but she was curious.

She decided to keep a closer eye on her younger brother.

For his part, Christopher thought it was exciting to have such a big secret. He thought about the gargoyles all day, wherever he was, at school or at home. In the mornings, he opened his window and waved down into the park. Ambergine was always standing there waiting for him and waved back. Christopher loved walking by the park gates to go to school, especially when Ambergine grinned at him or even when Gargoth stuck out his tongue and scowled.

One morning Claire almost caught Gargoth in the act, but then decided she was seeing things and dragged Christopher more quickly along, with a few concerned backward glances.

Every night before bed, Christopher opened his bedroom window and played guitar out into the cold night air. He was almost always applauded by one gargoyle gently clapping, and even very occasionally, if he played *really* well, by the sound of two gargoyles gently clapping.

The gargoyles were his special secret.

Each day after school Katherine and Christopher chatted, cleaned up apple cores, switched the stone gargoyles, and walked Marbles together. One day on a dog walk, Katherine turned to Christopher and stopped him.

"I'm glad that you moved into the house next door to the park," she said. "It's good that we can trust the person who lives there. You can help us keep the gargoyles safe."

Christopher nodded. "Yeah. I like it too. I mean, I'm happy to be able to keep an eye on them, too," he said. He felt fiercely loyal to Katherine, Cassandra, and the gargoyles at that moment.

He knew two things, then and there.

One, he'd never let anyone hurt Gargoth and Ambergine, not if he could help it.

And two, he was becoming fast friends with them all …

… which is why the next part of this story is so very sad.

Chapter Nineteen
The Statue in the Window

James stretched his legs out under his desk, avoiding his chemistry homework. He laced his hands behind his head and looked out his bedroom window, where the first snow of the year was gently falling. The snow was filling all the little backyards that crisscrossed behind James's house, falling onto dozens of yards and empty spaces behind all the houses and apartment buildings in the neighbourhood.

James had been home for months now, back into the world of school, homework, his home life with his parents in Toronto. He missed his grandfather and his sunny English garden, though.

He'd been thinking about the gargoyles, too. What did they do in the snowy weather?

Septimus wouldn't have any leaves to pile up, and Arabella wouldn't have any more apples to throw at people. He chuckled at the thought. "I hope she doesn't learn about snowballs," he said to himself.

Theodorus loved the pond, but what did he do when it was frozen over? James looked at the little carved gargoyle that Theodorus had given him. It sat in his windowsill.

James liked to lie on his bed and look at the gargoyle in the window. At night, he shone his desk light on the statue, and it cast a large shadow on the wall beside his bed. The shadow gargoyle had wings, pointed ears, and a squat, leathery body.

The statue and its shadow made James feel like Septimus (for the statue looked most like him) was in his bedroom with him, come to life on his wall. James illuminated the gargoyle in his window every night as he was going to sleep, just to feel a little closer to his grandfather and to the creatures he had come to know so well.

James had to admit it: he missed the gargoyles. He couldn't talk to anyone about them either, since his dad and mom didn't know about them, and Grampa Gregory made him promise not to tell anyone. It was hard not to have anyone to share them with.

James tried to concentrate on his chemistry notes, but something was missing. He sighed and looked out the window into the snowy backyard again. He would have dearly welcomed the gentle flutter of an apple tree leaf upon the page of his chemistry book, or a splash of pond water in his face.

At that very moment, he wouldn't even have minded if a well-thrown apple bounced right off the top of his head.

Chapter Twenty
The Snowy Footsteps

One gently snowy evening in December, Christopher sat beside his open bedroom window, looking down into the park. He had found a small spotlight in the basement and asked Claire to help him install it in his window. He switched it on, and the golden light shone down into the park, lighting a circle of snow at the base of the apple tree.

The golden spotlight also glinted and shone on four beautiful snow statues.

Once the snow started to fall a few weeks earlier, Christopher had noticed snow sculptures appearing in the park, a new one every few days.

The first sculpture was of a strong boy, with a sack over his shoulder. He looked sad and old-fashioned, as though he came from a long time ago and had walked a long, long way on weary feet.

A second snow statue appeared a few days later, and was a beautiful lion with its left ear broken off. It was regal and fierce but somehow looked very ancient.

Then in a few more days, a third snow statue appeared. It was a young girl kicking a soccer ball. The snow sculpture looked a lot like Katherine.

The most recent sculpture was of Christopher himself playing guitar. They were beautiful works of art, and Gargoth had made them all.

Christopher admired the snow statues in the soft spotlight from his window. Then he picked up his guitar and began playing into the night. Snow was falling delicately, softening and quieting the busy city.

His music lifted through the snowy air.

Ambergine came out of the bushes first and stepped into the spotlight near the apple tree (still magically bearing fruit). She looked up at the boy in the window and did a little curtsy. Then she started spiralling and pirouetting in the snow, dancing to the guitar music (she was amazingly dainty, for a gargoyle). Slowly, reluctantly, Gargoth joined her (he couldn't help himself), and there in the snowy, strange little gothic park, Christopher watched the two ancient creatures dance and pirouette and move together in a gargoyle ballet as the snow fell gently upon them.

Christopher loved the ritual of the night-time guitar serenade, but he had to be careful, because Gargoth had discovered (through peeking out of the bushes and watching the older Cannings) that snow could be patted into a ball and used as a very effective projectile. Christopher never knew if a "snow apple" was going to whiz at him as he played guitar. He had to keep a sharp eye out, but that was happening less and less these days. More often, Gargoth would sit beneath the apple tree and look at his snow sculptures, quietly smoking his pipe, listening to the guitar music.

After Christopher finished his song, he waved at Ambergine (Gargoth had already disappeared back into the bushes), turned off the spotlight, then closed the window. As he lay in his bed, he couldn't help grinning. The world was a great place.

He loved Toronto and his new friends.

The next morning, he woke and opened his window to wave good morning to Ambergine ... and saw a terrible sight.

Two gargoyles lay smashed to pieces at the base of the apple tree! Christopher's heart sped up to a painful thudding in his chest.

It's just the statues, isn't it? Yes, it must be!

Christopher forced himself to look carefully over the park ... and gasped. The apple tree was gone! It lay ruined in the snow where someone had chopped it down. Apples lay everywhere. Christopher stared in horror ... his special park was a ruined mess, and heavy human footprints trampled the fresh snow, all around.

Christopher ran downstairs, jumped into Marc's much-too-big work boots, and burst out the back door. Marbles flew out the door with him, and boy and dog ran through the snow and along the park fence to the gates. Cassandra was standing there in a long cloak, peering into the park. She patted Marbles, who wagged his tail and banged his head into her knees.

"Cassandra! The gargoyles! What happened?" Christopher was breathless, realizing at that very moment that he was standing at the gates in his pyjamas. A streetcar rolled by and he noticed people pointing at him. He started shivering. Cassandra took off her warm cloak and put it on his shoulders, which was strangely comforting.

"I don't know where they are. They're gone, though. I've called and called them," she said.

Christopher peered into the park. The smashed stone gargoyles lay in pieces at the stump of the apple tree. The tree itself lay shedding apples on the ground. He looked up at the park gates, now so barren without their gargoyles, living or stone.

"Who would break the stone gargoyle statues? Who would cut down a living tree?" he asked, his lips shivering, although he was no longer cold.

"Can't you guess?" Cassandra asked calmly.

"Well, vandals could do it, somebody angry," Christopher said, knowing it wasn't vandals.

"Yes, somebody angry. But no, not vandals, Christopher, although that might actually be nicer than the alternative. No, I'm afraid the Collector has seen his chance and surprised the gargoyles in their sleep, even though one of them is usually awake to keep watch. He's broken the stone statues and chopped down the tree in a rage." She looked down sadly at the boy beside her.

"We can only hope that our friends escaped," she added quietly.

Christopher grasped Marbles by the collar and said in a fierce voice, "The Collector is not going to hurt them, because I won't let him!" She laid a hand on his shoulder.

"They may be at Katherine's," she said.

There was hope, then.

Christopher ran to his house to get dressed. Since it was Saturday, most of his family was out shopping. Someone always needed to buy something in a big family. Claire was at home, though, studying for a big chemistry test. When he whipped past her room on his way out, she jumped up and ran after him, saying, "What's happening, C.C.? What's the rush?" but her little brother didn't even slow down to answer her. She stood at the back door holding Marbles by the collar, watching Christopher dash through the snow, across the street and into Candles by Daye.

"Hmm. I'm going to have to pay that store a visit," Claire said to Marbles as she shut the door. Marbles whined, wagged his tail, and lay down in his bed by the back door.

Christopher burst into the store with a loud tinkle of the shop bell. It had a "Closed" sign hanging in the window, but the door was open for him. He heard Cassandra say on the phone. "Okay then, Christopher can start looking. Maybe they haven't gone very far."

His heart sank. Cassandra hung up and leaned on the counter, pushing her curly red hair out of her face. "Well, they aren't at Katherine's," she said.

"Where could they be?"

Cassandra shook her head. "It's a big city, Christopher, but if they had any choice, they would stay close to us. Is Marbles any good at tracking?" Christopher's dog had never tracked anything in his life. He was really good at discovering dropped crumbs under the table, though.

"I don't know. Maybe. He's got a good nose for food."

"Well, let's bring him along. Let him sniff the statues. Maybe he can help us somehow. Meet me at the gates in a few minutes. I have to make one more phone call."

Christopher left the store to get his dog, and Cassandra grew solemn. She had to call the police, and she wasn't sure what, exactly, to tell them. "Hello, Officer, I've lost my gargoyles, oh, and they're alive," just wasn't really an option.

She tapped in the number. "Yes, officer? An emergency? No, no. Well. Yes. But no. Not really. Our park has been vandalized. Yes. Two antique stone statues were smashed last night. Expensive? Well, they were worth a bit, but not priceless. They'd be impossible to replace, though. And someone cut down an apple tree. Living? Yes, it was living, it had apples on it. It was rare, a Cellini apple tree. Do I know who did it? Well, I have an idea …"

Cassandra gave a very thorough description of the Collector and agreed to meet the police officer at the park gates in a few minutes. She wanted the police to be looking for him everywhere.

Someone had to stop the Collector. She and Katherine had already saved Gargoth from the old man once. She wanted more than anything to protect both gargoyles from harm, but harm had found them again, anyway, which seemed so unfair.

Where would they *ever* be safe?

A police car stopped in front of the park. Cassandra locked her store and crossed the street to join the officer stepping out of the car. Christopher was waiting there too, with Marbles on his leash. Cassandra and the police officer started chatting, and the officer took out a huge key and unlocked the gate. For the first time since moving into the neighbourhood, Christopher walked through the wide open front gates of the park. It felt strange.

The two adults and the boy and his dog looked around the park. Big, heavy footprints marked the snow. Apples lay all around and looked as though they'd been thrown there, some smashed to pieces.

As they approached the apple tree, Christopher could see the two statue gargoyles lying in ruins. One of the gargoyles was missing a wing and the other lay in two pieces, its head broken away from its body.

Both statues were so lifeless and dead-looking, staring into the sky.

Christopher shuddered. The gargoyles he knew were so alive, so individual and interesting. They talked to him and listened to his music. They threw snowballs, made ice sculptures, and danced in the snow. He didn't want to imagine Ambergine and Gargoth lying in the snow somewhere, staring and lifeless like the statues, but he couldn't help it. He shuddered again.

He suddenly realized how much danger his friends were in.

Marbles snuffled through the snow at his feet and sniffed all around the stump of the apple tree. It was almost as though the dog knew that something bad had happened. Christopher let him sniff. Maybe his dog would surprise them all and do something useful.

Cassandra and the police officer were talking, when a tall newspaper reporter joined them. His name was Stern and he was from the local newspaper, *The East End Crier*. Stern bounced on the balls of his feet and was altogether too chipper and eager.

Christopher liked him immediately.

Stern asked Christopher and Cassandra a lot of

questions, poked around the fountain and the bushes, took a few photographs and Cassandra's business card, then left. Then the police officer left too, relocking the gate behind him (Cassandra showed him the hidden doorway, which he found fascinating). As the police car pulled away, a taxi drove up to the park gates and stopped. Katherine got out and walked through the doorway into the park.

"You just missed the police *and* a newspaper reporter," Christopher said.

"My mom and dad are looking for them around our house," she said, ignoring him. She stuck her hands into her pockets. She sniffled. Christopher could see she had tears in her eyes. Cassandra seemed deep in thought, staring at the broken statues at her feet. Katherine walked away for a moment then let out a little cry. Christopher ran over and cried out too: Gargoth's beautiful snow sculptures were ruined. The statue of the old-fashioned boy, the regal lion, the girl playing soccer, the boy with the guitar, all were now just lumps of trampled snow.

"Why would the Collector destroy the snow statues, too?"

"Because they were beautiful, and because Gargoth made them," Katherine said sadly.

Christopher had never felt so joyless in his life. It seemed that everything sweet and beautiful lay in ruins at his feet.

Cassandra broke into their thoughts. "That reporter, Stern, is going to print a story and photos about this park. It will be in the local paper and on their website on Monday, and it will have a description of the Collector in it," she said.

"That's good, isn't it?" Christopher asked. "I mean, it's good if people are looking for him. If they know he wrecked the park?"

"Yes, it's good that lots of people keep an eye out for him. We need all the help we can get. But he's cunning and slippery, and he's going to do everything he can not to get caught," Cassandra answered. "One thing's for sure: this little park is headline news now. It was locked and abandoned for so long, people had mostly forgotten about it. According to Stern, the city isn't sure what to do with it, and some developer wants to make it into apartments or something. Whatever happens now, it won't be forgotten for long. And it's no longer safe for our friends when we find them."

Christopher was grateful that Cassandra didn't say "if," that would have been too much to bear. The three friends grew silent, each lost in thought.

Where were the gargoyles? Did the Collector have them? How were they going to find them in this enormous city?

Christopher was kicking his boot into the snow when suddenly Marbles gave a big tug on his leash, straining toward the back of the park. He started barking and acting crazy.

"What is it, Marbles?" Christopher let his dog drag him through the snow. Marbles leaped into a bush, pulling Christopher off his feet so hard that he dropped the leash. His dog lunged at something, growling and barking. Suddenly, a man jumped out of the bushes.

It was the Collector!

Christopher gasped and shouted, "YOU!" He struggled to get to his feet in the slippery snow.

Then everything happened so fast.

Marbles sank his teeth into the old man's pant leg and tugged and tugged, growling and shaking his head back and forth. The Collector kept his balance, kicking and shaking his leg, grunting, "Let go of me, stupid dog!"

Cassandra and Katherine were at Christopher's side in a second, astonished at what Marbles had found in the bushes. But before anyone could do anything, the old man yanked his pant leg out of Marbles' mouth and fell over the park fence. He loped to the road and sped off in the waiting taxi Katherine had just left. He was amazingly spry, it was almost unnatural.

"Where are they, you monster!" Katherine yelled after him. But the Collector was gone. Christopher grabbed Marbles' leash before he could leap the fence and run after the taxi.

"He was here the whole time?" Christopher said in disbelief.

"No, no, it's good," Katherine said. "Don't you see? He doesn't know where the gargoyles are either. He doesn't have them, or why would he be lurking around here?"

"You're right, Katherine! The first good news we've had today," Cassandra answered.

But it didn't help the friends feel much better. If the gargoyles weren't with the evil old man, and not in the park, then where could they be?

Chapter Twenty-Two
Lost Again

Gargoth woke and blinked. He was lying face up in the snow. His body felt like ice, and he ached all over. He stood and tried his wings.

Not broken. But useless. His left wing was in tatters. A sharp stick poked up through the snow and was lodged in the thin, leathery skin.

He winced and gently removed the stick, trying his wings again. Shredded, his left wing hung painfully. He wasn't going anywhere, not in the air, anyway.

It was night time. He shook his head and tried to clear his thoughts. He needed to find out where he was but he couldn't remember anything.

What had happened? Where was Ambergine?

He gingerly climbed into a tree, trying not to bang his damaged wing.

He looked out over a cemetery, a very old one. It was small and quiet, but he could see a road with cars not far off. There were bank towers behind that, so he was still in the city. That was good. He scanned the skyline, but he couldn't see the CN Tower. He wasn't exactly sure where he was.

A horse whinnied nearby. He could smell animals, too. Farm animals. In the city? How could that be? He would look around in the daylight, but he was too tired and dazed to do it now.

He struggled to a crook in the tree and propped himself there.

He was lost, hurt, and alone.

Even the hot tears coursing down his fat, leathery cheeks couldn't warm him.

Chapter Twenty-Three
Come Out, Come Out

It was a few weeks before the holidays, and Cassandra's store was packed with shoppers. Katherine and Christopher spent the rest of that day looking for the gargoyles, alone.

They went through the dog park ravine, calling and looking up into the trees. They had to be careful; they didn't want to attract any attention. It was a little odd calling up into trees in a Toronto park. One concerned dog owner asked if they'd lost a parakeet or some other precious pet bird?

"No, no!" said Katherine. "We're looking for our ..." She drew a complete blank and couldn't think of a single thing to say except "gargoyle." The truth just wasn't an option.

Christopher broke in, "We're looking for our cat. She ran off this morning in this direction."

The owner was a little surprised that any cat owner would go searching for her lost pet with a huge dog like Marbles in tow, but eventually they convinced him that Marbles *loved* cats.

They tried to be more careful then and called up into the trees quietly, one at a time. After a while they gave up at the park and walked through the neighbourhood, all along the tree-lined streets, quietly calling up into the trees and rooftops.

"I see Gargoth! I see him!" Christopher yelled as he pointed up into a huge Chinese elm tree.

But alas, "Gargoth" turned out to be a very large, grouchy raccoon, woken from its sleep in the crook of a branch. It hissed at Christopher then ambled away to a higher and more private part of the colossal tree.

"I can't believe how many trees there are in Toronto!" Christopher started to complain. It was getting dark, and both he and Katherine were tired. It was time to return home.

"They will be getting hungry. I wonder if there are any apple orchards nearby?" Katherine said. Christopher shrugged. He really didn't know enough about Toronto to say.

"I'll check the Internet when I get home tonight," Katherine said with a giant yawn. "Toronto must have some orchards somewhere, right? It used to be all farms, not that long ago."

They went back to Cassandra's store, which was just closing for the evening. Their faces told her everything she needed to know: no luck.

Cassandra tried to sound hopeful. "We'll keep looking. We'll find them. I'll put the candles out on the rooftop tonight," she said. "At least we can light their way home if they're searching for us."

Christopher went home immediately, promising to return early the next day. Katherine waited for her dad to come and pick her up from the store. She couldn't wait until he got there though: it was a sad and empty place without Gargoth and Ambergine in it.

When they had gone, Cassandra lugged a huge box to the rooftop. It was her box of leftover candles from years of sales, and it was filled with smiling Halloween pumpkin candles, Christmas tree candles, pirate skull candles, CN Tower candles, and every possible candle you can imagine. She carefully arranged 148 of the mismatched candles in a giant circle, with two diamonds, one on top of the other, inside it. It looked like this:

If the gargoyles were flying above the city, lost and searching, they would see Cassandra's beacon of candles. It was their stonemason's mark calling them home, and had one candle for every year they were parted from each other.

When morning came, kind Cassandra was asleep under a blanket on the roof, with Halloween pumpkins and Christmas trees and skulls and CN Tower candles burnt out, all around her.

Chapter Twenty-four
Snake at the Tree

The next day was snowy and cold. Cassandra's store was filled with holiday shoppers looking for the perfect gift (a set of healing chime balls or a skull bandana perhaps), so she was too busy to help search for the lost friends. Katherine and Christopher would again have to look for the gargoyles on their own. They decided to split up to cover more ground.

Katherine found a few parks with apple trees in them because they had once been farms, many years before the city grew up around them. She and her mother were going to look there, in her part of town.

Christopher decided to continue the search around his neighbourhood, up and down more tree-lined streets.

He put on a heavy coat and boots and his favourite red wool cap and headed out into the snow. Before he started his search he wanted to take one more careful look at the park. It was hard to go back in there without his friends, but he couldn't shake the feeling that he was missing something, some important clue. He stood by the gates until the sidewalk was clear of people for a moment, then he pushed open the little hidden door and slipped through. The park was quiet, except for the bubbling of the fountain. He walked through the thick snow and looked around.

The falling snow was making white peaks on the bushes and the fallen apple tree. The benches were covered with snow, and the broken stone gargoyles were slowly being covered by a soft white blanket. It seemed that no one had the heart to clean them up.

Christopher's stomach lurched violently as he looked at the broken statues. He turned away. He couldn't bear to see them smashed in the snow.

He walked around, not exactly sure what he was looking for. He poked his head into the bushes and around the back of the park fence, but didn't find anything to tell him where his lost gargoyle friends might be. He was about to give up and leave …

… when a voice spoke from the tree.

"They're gone." It was a man's voice.

Christopher stood stock still. His eyes took in the tree, but there was nothing to see.

"Who's there?" he called.

"Don't you want to see your friends again?" the voice said. "I know where they are."

It was a silky smooth voice that sounded like venom and lies.

Christopher watched in horror as a figure slowly rose from the snow next to the stump of the apple tree.

It was an old man with thick glasses, a white straw hat, and a heavy brown coat, and he'd been sitting in the snow, waiting. Christopher had seen him before but wasn't expecting to see him again so soon.

It was the Collector.

Christopher looked around, but there was no one to help him. No Marbles, no Cassandra, no Katherine. He looked at his house next door with cheerful lights on, some of his family inside, but they wouldn't hear him call. His heart started pounding painfully, but there was something else too: a sudden flicker of anger.

"Where are they then?" Christopher shouted. "I don't believe you. You don't know where the gargoyles are, or you wouldn't be here looking for them!"

The Collector gave a greasy smile. His glasses were so thick that Christopher couldn't see his eyes, which was a bit of a distraction.

"Oh, I'm not looking for them. I'm here looking for you, Christopher Canning."

Christopher gulped.

What could the Collector want with *him*?

"Why me? Why are you looking for me? How do you know my name?" Christopher hadn't moved, but he was eyeing the park fence nearby. He was wondering how quickly he could run there and jump over it.

"You live right next door. It's not hard to find out your name, Christopher. And the other two, that Daye person and the Katherine girl, they won't talk to me or let me in that awful store. Most unreasonable, really." The Collector flicked a snowflake from the shoulder of his brown wool jacket and flashed his toothy smile at Christopher. His fingernails were long and yellow, with a kind of animal look to them, like someone who wasn't in the habit of showing them to people very often.

"But you seem like a sensible boy. Someone who might be persuaded to listen to reason." The old man's voice was like oily soup — it made Christopher want to gag.

"What do you want then? Hurry up!" Christopher tried to sound calm, but he was yelling. The Collector sidled closer to him, looking casual and unhurried.

"You're right. I don't know where BOTH of the gargoyles are. I do know where ONE of them is, though. I assure you she is safe and sound. So you'll believe me, here's a picture."

The old man tossed an envelope into the snow at Christopher's feet. The boy picked it up and shakily drew out the photo. It was a picture of Ambergine, and she was holding onto the bars of a cage, looking angrily at the camera.

"You … you have Ambergine locked in a CAGE?" Christopher said. He felt his skin crawling with anger. Before he knew what he was doing he ran at the Collector, but the old man stepped aside. He was surprisingly nimble. Christopher tripped and sprawled into the snow. He was so angry, tears were streaking down his face.

The old man's voice grew cold and menacing. He leaned over Christopher in the snow and snarled in his ear, "Yes, I have her in a nice cage, where she is safe and sound. But she's not what I want. What I really want is the other one, Gargoth. He is mine, my father paid for him, and I want him back. He's *my* property, and your thieving friends stole him from me. I'm prepared to make a switch. The female gargoyle can have her freedom, but I want Gargoth in exchange."

Christopher picked himself up from the snow and stared at the old man in disbelief.

The Collector smiled again, which made Christopher recoil, and continued in his slimy voice. "All you have to do is find him and bring him to me, and the other one can go free."

"You're crazy!" Christopher shouted. "You're the thief! And I would never give Gargoth to you! We'll find Ambergine and save her from you ourselves."

The Collector cracked his awful smile again and moved toward the park gates. "Oh, I think you'll do as I say. You'll find Gargoth and bring him here and hand him over to me, or the girl gargoyle will live in the cage forever, and you wouldn't want that now, would you?"

Christopher was filled with revulsion as the old man opened the hidden doorway. He continued in his cold voice. "Leave a lit candle in the park when you find him, as a signal. Oh, and if I find out you've told your friends that I have the girl gargoyle, she dies."

Christopher's knees felt weak.

Dies?

Katherine told him that the horrible old man would stop at nothing to get Gargoth back, but would he actually *kill* Ambergine? He watched the evil man stoop through the hidden doorway and disappear along the sidewalk, vanishing among the throng of holiday shoppers. Christopher stood a long time in the snow, tears slowly freezing to his face.

How could *anyone* be so cruel?

Chapter Twenty-five
Still Lost

Gargoth woke with a start. He distinctly heard a horse neigh and children laugh somewhere nearby. The sun was overhead, shining right into his eyes. He shook and tried to stretch in the tree, but his torn wing hurt too much for him to move.

What had happened? How did he get there? Where was Ambergine?

He tried to remember, but it was foggy. He slowly lit his pipe and tried to think …

… he and Ambergine were in the park. Christopher had been playing his guitar, and they had danced in the snow. The boy waved good night, then …

… then … then there was a loud smash! Someone had thrown something heavy at the base of the tree! Then again, something heavy smashed into the tree.

He and Ambergine were startled awake, frightened … and … and …

… the tree fell!

Gargoth sat up very straight. Everything about that terrible night suddenly came back to him. He had fallen asleep! It was his turn to keep watch while Ambergine slept, but he had *dozed off.*

He fell asleep next to Ambergine, and the Collector found a quiet way into the park. He must have used the hidden doorway. Then two heavy hands had grabbed Ambergine from the tree before either of them knew what was happening!

Gargoth groaned with agony and shame and dropped his heavy head into his claws.

He remembered now.

The Collector had grabbed Ambergine and locked her in a cage. The last time Gargoth had seen that cage, it was dangling from a pole along with the Collector, from the roof of his creepy mansion. Gargoth shuddered and willed himself not to think about that terrible place.

He had to concentrate.

What had happened to Ambergine?

Gargoth had thrown apples at the old man, then snow apples. He attacked the Collector again and again and again with whatever he could find, but the Collector ran off laughing, with the cage and Ambergine locked inside. They vanished into a waiting taxi which zoomed away with Ambergine screaming and screaming from her cage: "*Fly, Gargoth, fly!*"

And he did fly, as fast as he could, as far as he could. He followed the taxi as it sped away. He flew his fastest, but it wasn't fast enough, and the taxi and Ambergine vanished in the distance. He didn't stop flying until he must have collapsed from exhaustion, and fell from the skies into the snow. Which brought him right here.

Wherever this was.

Gargoth shook himself then huddled deeper into the notch of the tree. He would never be warm or whole, ever again. He had fallen asleep and failed Ambergine.

It was his fault that she was gone, and he really didn't care if he lived or died.

Chapter Twenty-Six
C.C. Tells the Truth

Claire Canning was studying at her desk. She had a chemistry test the next day, and although chemistry wasn't particularly hard for her, she found it dull studying so much. She kept peering out her bedroom window onto the street a bit too often.

That is how she saw her little brother in his red wool cap emerge from the park next door. She had been noticing him spending quite a lot of time in the park, day and night, which was odd, since as far as she could tell there really wasn't anything of interest for a twelve-year-old boy in there. As he emerged through the gate, his hands were dug deep into his pockets, and his shoulders were hunched in a way that suggested tears and upset. She watched him cross the street and stand in front of the old store, Candles by Daye, hesitating. He seemed so unsure and small and vulnerable that Claire put down her pencil. Chemistry could wait.

Christopher needed a friend. He pushed open Cassandra's shop door and breathed in the familiar scent of cinnamon and incense. The store was surprisingly full of holiday shoppers. There was a line-up at the cash register with people eager to buy Buddha statues and hanging bead curtains, and Cassandra was very busy tending to everyone.

She was saying, "Dragon candlesticks? Over by the far window," to a lady with two small children, as she was wrapping a box of Christmas tree candles for a middle-aged man. A pair of teenagers stood by a display of bandanas and skeleton necklaces, laughing.

Christopher felt overwhelmed. The store was usually a nice quiet place, a haven, and he was upset that it was so busy, especially after what had just happened in the park. Cassandra looked up and smiled at him, but she was too busy to talk.

He felt terrible. What was he going to do? The Collector had Ambergine somewhere in the city, and he couldn't tell his friends about it.

He dug his hands into his pockets. He had so longed for a secret, and here was one he really didn't want. The worst kind of secret, one where someone could get hurt or worse. It wasn't fair. He suddenly felt much too young to be involved. All he had wanted was a friend, and here he was weighed down by an awful secret.

He wandered to a quieter part of the store by the self-help books and picked up a discounted pumpkin candle left over from Halloween. His eyes filled with tears ...

... when the store door opened, the little bell tinkled, and in walked Claire. She saw him, smiled, and walked over to him, only to find her little brother awash in tears.

"Christopher, what is it? Are you hurt?" She was suddenly worried.

But he shook his head and darted a look at Cassandra at the cash register. "No, we should go, though." He turned and fled from the store.

Claire followed. Christopher started to run down the sidewalk, but Claire caught up to him and grabbed his arm. "Christopher! C.C.! Stop! You have to tell me. What's wrong? What's happened?" He looked at his sister and felt a tiny glimmer of hope.

The Collector had said he couldn't tell his *friends* about Ambergine ... but Claire was his *sister*. The Collector hadn't said anything about *her*. He dried his eyes with his mitten and looked over at the park.

"Okay, I'll tell you. But you have to promise, PROMISE, not to tell anyone else. Not Mom and Dad. Not Marc. Not anyone else. And it's going to sound ... well, crazy, I guess."

Claire nodded, a little worried. Her brother wasn't usually so intense. Brother and sister walked across the street through the hidden park doorway (which Claire loved), and into the park. Christopher settled Claire on the bench at the stump of the apple tree. He paced in the snow before her and started a strange story. If Claire didn't know her brother better, she would have said it was made up.

But her little brother rarely made up stories, so she had no choice but to believe it.

It was amazing, it was unbelievable, but there were the broken statues, and the ruined apple tree somehow full of fruit in the middle of the winter. Claire nodded and hemmed and hawed, and when her brother had finished his story, she knew what she had to do.

She promised Christopher that his secret was safe with her.

But her idea of safe was very different from his.

No one threatened her little brother and got away with it. And in her experience of the world, most secrets were evil things that only helped protect bad people and hurt innocent ones.

Claire Canning wasn't one for keeping secrets, at least not the kind that frightened children.

She grasped her brother by the mittened hand and said, "Come on, C.C.," purposefully marching across the little park.

"Where are we going?" he gasped, keeping up.

"I think it's time for you to introduce me to Cassandra Daye."

But Claire was thinking, *And I hope she knows how to keep a secret better than you do.*

Chapter Twenty-Seven
In the Cage

Ambergine woke and groaned softly. Her entire body hurt from head to taloned toe, and from wingtip to wingtip. She slowly opened her eyes and tried to focus.

There were bars in front of her face. She was in a cage! It was cramped and uncomfortable, and she longed to stretch her wings and shake herself, but there wasn't room. She made herself stay calm and look around. She was in an old house. Somewhere nearby, perhaps downstairs, a baby was crying. She wished she could soothe it, but she wasn't in any shape to help another creature at the moment.

Her cage was in a room with an indoor water pump (although she vaguely knew that it wasn't called a water pump), an indoor cooking fire (she knew it wasn't called that, either), and a food box (with another name she couldn't recall). She thought it might be in the room that humans called a "kitchen." It was sparse, without any furniture or hangings on the walls. Her cage was beside a window, looking down into a tiny, snowy backyard and the many small yards and kitchen windows of neighbouring houses.

The yard had soil underneath the new blanket of snow. That's all she needed.

The sun was coming up. Ambergine didn't know how much time she had before her captor appeared, so she had to act quickly. She was close enough to the window to push it with her claw. She reached through the bars of her cage and pushed and pushed against the window, as quietly as she could until the window opened a crack. She reached into her pouch and pulled out an apple: her last Cellini apple from the park.

She put the apple to her gargoyle lips inhaling the familiar scent, then breathed out slowly. She had one shot, and it had better be a good one. She wished she was Gargoth, because HE never missed. Carefully she took aim then tossed the apple through the window. She watched it bounce on the balcony railing, totter, then tumble slowly over…

… and roll into the snow of the tiny backyard, landing with a gentle "shoosh."

She could watch over the apple now. It was her only hope.

Chapter Twenty-Eight
The East End Crier

It was Monday morning. James pulled himself out of bed, opened his curtains, and looked into his backyard. Big snowfall yesterday. Big chemistry test today. He picked up Theodorus's gargoyle statue and rubbed its head.

"Hope you can watch over me today, little guy, bring me luck on my chemistry test!" He replaced the statue carefully in the window and went to get ready for school.

When he got downstairs, his father was reading the local paper, *The East End Crier*, at the kitchen table. His mother had already left for work. James looked over his father's shoulder as he reached for the milk carton on the table and stopped dead.

"Vandals Smash Gargoyles!" the newspaper headline shouted. He grabbed the paper from his father, who complained and read the short article out loud:

An abandoned park in the east end was vandalized on Saturday night. Two antique stone gargoyles were smashed and a rare Cellini apple tree was cut down. Local resident and shop owner, Cassandra Daye, who owns the curio store Candles by Daye, reported the crime, stating the antique statues would be impossible to replace and the Cellini apple tree is very rare. Residents are asked to contact police if they have any further information.

The article was written by a reporter named Stern, and it went on to describe the location of the park. What really made James stare were the photographs: the park had a fountain, an apple tree, and one of the photos showed the head of a broken statue.

It was a *gargoyle*!

He looked in amazement then got his father's magnifying glass from the writing desk and looked more closely. Suddenly, he realized he looked exactly like his grandfather examining newspapers all summer.

But the magnifying glass really did help him see everything in the grainy images. James peered at the photographs. There were footprints in the snow all around the smashed statues.

"I wonder ..." James stood at the dining room table, scratching his head.

His father called him from the front hall. "Come on, Jamie! If you want a ride to school, you'd better hurry!"

James stuffed the newspaper into his backpack, grabbed an apple for breakfast, and dashed out the door to his father's car.

After school and his chemistry test (which he did rather well on, he thought), James jumped on the streetcar. He quickly found the little park described in the newspaper, and not long afterwards he stood on the sidewalk looking in through the park gates.

It was locked, but that wasn't going to stop him. He was definitely too big to squeeze through the bars, but he was big enough to jump over the fence at the back of the park. The snow was thick, and the bushes dumped their snow as he vaulted over the iron railing (he left the sidewalk, since he didn't want anyone to see him). He slowly walked to the centre of the tiny place.

He approached the fallen apple tree.

"It's bearing fruit," he said to himself as he touched an apple. He noticed how beautiful the tree was — he'd never seen anything like it. The fruit was golden and sweet-smelling, and still warm to the touch, even lying in the snow.

He walked over to the seahorse fountain, which was bubbling away quietly. "Hmm. Water." He walked to the tree stump and started snapping photos on his cell phone. After brushing away the snow, he took several pictures of the broken gargoyle statues, and several close-ups of their faces.

"Grampa Gregory will definitely want to see this," he said under his breath as he snapped photo after photo.

The snow covered many of the tracks, and people had come and gone since the statues were broken and the tree cut down.

James kept looking. He pushed bushes aside, moving slowly along the fence, carefully looking over the snow. Finally, he let out a little gasp. There it was, he'd found it: a perfect undisturbed footprint in the snow.

It wasn't human. Oh no. It was just like Theodorus's wet print on the flagstones beside the summer pond.

It was the scaly, taloned imprint of a gargoyle.

CHapTer TWeNTY-NiNe
DOWN ON THE FARM

Katherine and Christopher were sick of looking up into city trees. They had spent days looking, straining to see up into the branches and treetops in street after street after street of tree-lined neighbourhoods. Their necks were sore from craning upward, their voices were hoarse from calling softly, and Katherine was developing a bad cold from standing out in the snowy sidewalks for so long. Occasionally, Claire had tagged along to help, but since she'd never met a gargoyle and didn't know Gargoth or Ambergine, she didn't really know what or who she was looking for.

Katherine's parents hadn't had any luck in their part of town, and Cassandra hadn't been able to help much due to the busy holiday season. She did keep the 148 mismatched candle beacon lit on the rooftop every night, though.

Katherine and Christopher had been shooed away by people suspicious of them lurking around their houses and looking up into the trees. They'd been chased by angry dogs and hissed at by more raccoons (there were a LOT of raccoons in Toronto, as well as trees, Christopher was dismayed to discover, all about the same size and shape as a gargoyle).

School was out for the holidays. They travelled the streetcar to a new area of the city each day, carrying the big yellow backpack in case they had any luck.

But they didn't.

On the plus side, they hadn't seen the Collector since he had threatened Christopher in the park. They had no idea where the awful old man had gone, though, which was scary too. He might pop out at them at any moment.

It is difficult to keep looking and looking without much hope of finding what you are looking for. Christopher was having trouble keeping his spirits up: the Collector had Ambergine in a cage.

It was a terrible secret to have to keep.

Katherine and Christopher were walking through a very old part of the city. It was so old that it held one of the city's oldest cemeteries AND the city's only working farm.

The pair walked along the snowy pathway and through the railed farm gates. The farm was a happy place for families, and lots of little children were running around in their snowsuits, making snow angels and looking through the wooden fence at the shaggy horse waiting patiently for its lunch of fresh hay. The piglets, chickens, roosters, rabbits, and other animals of the farm were inside the warm huts. There were parents and toddlers and strollers everywhere.

Katherine loved this farm, and she and her parents had come many times when she was little. She'd been one of the children running around in her snowsuit, patting the shaggy horse. Christopher couldn't believe that a huge city like Toronto had a farm in the middle of it.

Katherine looked at the farm map, but couldn't see an apple orchard marked anywhere. She thought there might be one, though, since the farm made and sold apple cider all winter long. She bought a cup from the vendor and shared the warm, spicy drink with Christopher.

"No wonder the gargoyles like apples, this is *good!*" he said, a little surprised.

A lady in a Toronto Parks employee jacket walked by, pushing an overflowing wheelbarrow filled with hay.

"Excuse me, can you point us in the direction of the apple orchard?" Katherine asked her. The lady put down the wheelbarrow and frowned.

"You know, we don't really have an orchard. There's an old apple tree behind the drive shed." She pointed down a narrow, snowy path with a shed at the end. "And there's another one out by the gate, but that's it. There might be an old apple orchard over in the Necropolis, though. That's right across the street."

"What about the cider?" Katherine asked.

"Oh, we get the apples for the cider from a lot of apple trees around the city, not just here. People pick them from parks and backyards and bring them here for us to use." Katherine thanked the lady, who picked up the wheelbarrow and trundled away, followed by squealing children who wanted to help feed the horse.

"What should we do now?" she asked.

Christopher shrugged. "I guess we try the Necropolis, whatever that is."

"It's a cemetery, Christopher. I think it means 'city of the dead,' actually," Katherine said.

They left the happy farm behind and crossed the street into a completely different world. The Necropolis was one of the oldest cemeteries in the city. It was an odd sensation, leaving the happy sounds of children feeding the horse, to the quiet dark of the waiting graveyard.

The cemetery wasn't very big and had once bordered on a farm, back in the 1850s. At the far eastern edge of the Necropolis they found a few old, gnarled apple trees, but it was hardly an orchard.

They wandered through the headstones, kicking the snow away along the path and looking up into the trees, gently calling. Christopher ran ahead and was looking at an interesting grave: Ned Hanlan, 1855–1908. As he finished reading about Ned Hanlan (a great oarsman and Canada's first world champion in any sport), he noticed a shiny headstone with an odd-looking angel on it. He walked over to it then realized it wasn't a headstone: it was a beautiful snow sculpture.

And it wasn't an angel, it was a gargoyle, and it looked like Ambergine!

"Katherine! C'mere!" he shouted.

"I've found a headstone!" he called. "I mean, a snow statue! A gargoyle!"

Katherine ran up and clasped him by the arm. "They must be here!" she cried.

The two plowed through the deep snow and called up into the trees. No gargoyle called back, though.

Then Katherine smelled familiar pipe smoke and ran down a small bushy path toward a large marble headstone ...

... where a little gargoyle was smoking a pipe, curled up next to a flying angel.

The gravelly voice said, "Bella grathen tador Ambe." There was no "hello" just the words, "Tell me you have found Ambergine?"

CHAPTER THIRTY
THE HIDDEN TURRET

Gargoth was growling and complaining.

Katherine and Christopher were on a crowded streetcar and Gargoth was inside the yellow canvas backpack, being bumped and jostled on Katherine's back. He was cramped and his sore wing was being crushed. He didn't seem to care if it was uncomfortable for Katherine, though, as he rolled and complained and jabbed her mercilessly with his pointed, taloned feet.

Gargoth growled. Gargoth sneezed. He grumbled in his strange, gravelly voice, "Behim mamot," which Katherine and Christopher both heard as, "Let me out!"

A small boy standing beside his mother looked up in shocked surprise, searching their faces. They both stared at him, until Katherine frowned and shook her head at him. The boy looked away quickly, but Christopher saw his eyes stray again and again to the yellow canvas backpack. They were both very relieved when the boy and his mother got off the streetcar.

"Shh! Gargoth, please," Katherine whispered over her shoulder. She really didn't want people to hear her backpack groaning and complaining. But Gargoth wasn't going to be quiet. The only thing he WAS quiet about was what happened in the park with the Collector. He wasn't very forthcoming about that night, or how he ended up in the Necropolis.

When Katherine had asked Gargoth about Ambergine, he went completely mute. He absolutely refused to mention her name or discuss her in any way.

Christopher started fidgeting.

Whatever Gargoth knew about Ambergine, he wasn't saying. Christopher could feel himself start to sweat.

It seemed like forever before he and Katherine and Gargoth finally got off the streetcar and stood in front of Cassandra's store. They both realized at the same time that they had a problem.

What, exactly, were they going to do with Gargoth?

Candles by Daye was swarming with people buying holiday gifts. Even if they wanted to push their way through the crowd buying dragon statues and skull candles, where would they take the gargoyle? Not to the rooftop, since the Collector might be watching from the library.

So Candles by Daye was out.

Katherine and Christopher looked over at the ruined park. After years of neglect, the park gates were open and it was suddenly swarming with people. City workers in colorful vests and hard hats were shovelling broken statue bits into the back of a city truck. Another worker was smoothing out the snow hills that were once snow statues.

A far worse thing was happening, though.

Two workmen were chain-sawing the branches off the destroyed apple tree. They were tossing the pieces into a wood chipper, which was spewing out apple tree bits into a bag at the back with a deafening roar.

It was horrifying. Katherine and Christopher both looked away. The park was overrun with people and everything was being shovelled or flattened or chipped. Clearly they couldn't leave Gargoth there, either.

"What are we going to do?" Katherine whispered.

"What about your house?" Christopher asked quietly. He pushed his glasses up his nose. He was getting nervous. He felt like the park workers were looking over at them.

"We could go to my house for now, but the Collector knows where I live," Katherine answered. She sounded nervous, too. A loud, gravelly voice from the backpack said, "I am NOT going back on that locomotion machine!"

Christopher was looking over at his house. The car wasn't in the garage, and there were no brothers or sister on the porch or playing hockey in the snowy driveway.

"Okay, we don't have any choice. Come on," he said.

They crossed the street and walked up to Christopher's front door. He listened carefully then put the key into the lock. He opened the door quietly and put his fingers to his lips.

"Shhh." He didn't know what Marbles would do if he found a *New Friend* entering the house AND smelled a *Wondrous Creature* in her backpack. He didn't want to find out either. They creaked up the stairs, past all the bedrooms, then quietly up to his turret.

Halfway up the stairs to his bedroom, Claire's door opened. She popped her head out, with Marbles at her knees.

She didn't get a word out. Marbles roared with delight at the sight of a *New Friend* and promptly knocked Claire to the ground. He bounded toward the stairs as Christopher yelled, "RUN!"

Katherine made it to the turret and slammed the door just as she heard the big dog hit the door behind her. There was much barking and scratching and the sound of both Claire and Christopher yelling, "No! No, Marbles! Down!"

"That was too close, Gargoth," Katherine whispered as she took off her backpack. She moved over to the window and looked down into the park. The workers were gone. The tree was gone. The statues were gone. The park was just a fence, a fountain, two benches, and some bushes.

Gargoth climbed gingerly out of the backpack and waddled over to her. Now she saw him indoors, he really did look damaged. His left wing was rumpled, the leathery skin pierced near the bottom, hanging in shreds.

"How did you do that?" she asked, pointing to his wing, but he refused to answer.

Instead, he climbed slowly into the window seat and looked down at the park below, but quickly turned away.

Christopher came into the room.

And so did Claire.

"Where's the dog?" Katherine asked, a little worried. (She was really more of a cat person.)

"Safely downstairs, locked in the kitchen," Christopher said.

Claire stepped forward. "Hi! I'm Claire!" she chirped.

"Hello," Katherine said, taken back by this cheerful teenager. Katherine didn't have any siblings and didn't know any girls a few years older than her. She was suddenly a little shy of Claire, who was tall and very grown up looking. She was dressed in jeans and a sweater, with an elegant flowery scarf around her neck.

"Hello, Gargoth. Sorry about Marbles," Claire said, turning to the little gargoyle with a smile. She crossed the room and knelt before him.

"Oh! Your poor wing!" She took off her flowery scarf and gently wrapped up Gargoth's wing, tying it with care at his neck. Katherine and Christopher held their breath: no one just walked up to Gargoth and wrapped up his wing.

Apparently, though, Claire Canning did. There was a quiet light in Gargoth's eye that Katherine hadn't seen before. He was staring at Claire with a calm look on his face.

"Do you live here?" he asked in gargoyle.

"One floor down, the bedroom beside the bathroom. You're always welcome to visit, just watch out for Marbles. I'm glad Katherine and Christopher found you, they've been looking for you every day for weeks. I'm pleased you've come, Gargoth of Tallus." Claire bent and kissed his head, then left the room.

Christopher and Katherine looked at each other, astonished.

Claire understood gargoyle language (a bit unusual for a teenager).

She wrapped up Gargoth's wing then *kissed* him and got away with it.

And Gargoth himself was gently stroking her flowery scarf as he climbed under a pile of clothes in Christopher's chair, where he went right to sleep.

You should also know Gargoth kept a scrap of that flowery scarf in his pouch from that day on, for years.

CHAPTER THIRTY-ONE
THE TRICKSTER

Ambergine's eyes flicked open. Her captor had entered the kitchen and was creeping quietly past her cage. It was too early for the sun to show its face. A baby was crying somewhere inside the house, again. It was a mournful sound, and she longed to soothe it.

She stayed completely still. The old man shuffled into the kitchen and over to the big box with food in it. He opened it and a dim light flickered. The light illuminated one side of the man's face. Ambergine saw his thick glasses (did he wear them in his sleep?) and shuddered. He looked evil, even in the half-light. He pulled a bottle out of the food box and got a cup from the shelf. He quietly poured himself a drink. Just as he was about to take a sip, Ambergine yelled out in gargoyle, "I'M THIRSTY!"

Her timing was perfect.

The old man dropped the cup and sprayed yellow liquid all over the kitchen. He snarled and turned toward her cage.

"Shut up! You don't say a word to me!" He drew his face close to the cage and stared at Ambergine. "I despise you. You cost me my gargoyle!"

Ambergine glowered back at him. "Gargoth is not *your* gargoyle, and neither am I," she said calmly. "And I'm not afraid of you, or your temper, or your obsession with Gargoth."

The Collector hissed. "Shut up! Shut up! You don't say his name to me!" He raised his hand and struck the top of the cage, which bounced wildly. Ambergine grasped the cage bars and bit her lip. The Collector could understand every word she said. Gargoth had never mentioned that he could understand their language.

It gave her strength, and an important edge. She knew what she had to do.

The Collector left the kitchen in a rage. She heard him stomp back up the stairs to what must be a sleeping compartment of some kind.

She was cramped and very uncomfortable in the cage. There was nothing she could do about that, though. She'd just have to cope until she could figure a way out. She knew that Gargoth had been locked in that cage for days, months, possibly even years at a time. The thought of him surviving in it for so long gave her strength.

She had spent most of her days and nights looking out the small window beside her. From her cage she could see snow-covered backyards and interesting houses and apartment buildings. People came and went below her on the icy garden paths and sidewalks.

At night, she peered intently into the lit windows of neighbouring houses, watching people writing at desks or eating dinner, or reading together as a family beside a cozy fire. It made her feel a little less lonely.

But none of the people in those houses knew that a little gargoyle was locked in a cage and watching them from a window high above.

Ambergine yawned and looked out into the backyard below. She gasped.

A small green apple tree leaf was poking through the snow.

Chapter Thirty-Two
The Note

Christopher, Katherine, and Cassandra were huddled around the countertop of Candles by Daye. They were studying a piece of paper.

It read: *"HAVE YOU FOUND HIM? LEAVE A LIT CANDLE IN THE PARK WHEN YOU DO."*

It was handwritten in black capital letters. When it arrived in his mailbox that morning, Christopher almost jumped out of his skin, but when he showed it to Claire, she was annoyingly calm.

"The Collector just doesn't want you to mention that he has Ambergine. You should show this note to your friends," Claire said. Christopher realized that Claire was right. It was a relief not to have to keep the Collector's horrible note a secret, too.

But now he had shown them, they weren't all that much help, since no one seemed to know what to do next.

"We HAVE found him, but why would we tell *him*? Why doesn't he ask about Ambergine, too?" Katherine mused. Christopher flinched, but Cassandra answered her.

"He only cares about Gargoth, Katherine. His father 'bought' Gargoth at a fairground when he was little, remember? He sees Gargoth as his property. He really doesn't care about Ambergine." Cassandra darted a look over at Christopher, who was carefully not making eye contact with anyone, then she went and busied herself straightening the store window.

Katherine was mad. It was SO unfair! When was the Collector going to leave them alone? She, Cassandra, and Ambergine had driven all the way to New York just a few months ago, found Gargoth, and saved him. They'd left the Collector clinging to a pole dangling from the rooftop of his mansion over a valley. She had dearly hoped he'd stay there.

"What are we going to do? Can't we just ignore him?" Katherine asked. She looked across the street at Christopher's house. They had left the gargoyle asleep in his bedroom. What if Gargoth woke up without them there and started wandering around the house? Marbles was safely locked up in the kitchen, but still ... with Gargoth, anything could happen. He wasn't used to living indoors.

Cassandra turned from the window, crossed her arms, and looked steadily at them both. "If we ignore him, Katherine, he's just going to keep bothering us. We'll never be rid of him, and neither will the gargoyles. There's only one thing we can do. We have to get rid of the Collector once and for all. And personally, I think he knows more about

Ambergine than he's saying." Cassandra looked at Christopher, who quickly looked away.

"There's no point just scaring him off or ignoring his demands, we have to stand up to him and get rid of him for good," she said finally.

"How?" Christopher asked, miserable.

Cassandra looked at him thoughtfully. "I'm not entirely sure yet, Christopher, but one thing is certain: we won't be able to get rid of him alone. We're going to need some help."

"Who's going to help us?"

But no matter how much Christopher asked, Cassandra wouldn't say another word.

Chapter Thirty-Three
The New Year's Party

The Cannings were having a holiday party. Not just any party, but a BIG party. Christopher's parents did this whenever they moved into a new house, so they could get to know their neighbours and co-workers, and so their children could invite new friends to their home.

This year was no different. Although Christopher and Claire weren't feeling particularly festive (and Gargoth was never in the mood for a party even at the best of times), they had no choice. Christopher's parents were used to having big parties on New Year's Eve, and this year wasn't going to be any different.

Christopher and Claire, their many-assorted-older-brothers, and their parents had spent all day decorating the house and trimming the outdoor pine trees (it was a big property, there were twelve trees in all). The front porch of the old house was filled with baskets overflowing with colourful pine cones and holly and berries and straw. There were lights and cedar boughs and a fire in the fireplace.

Even Marbles had a giant red bow tied around his neck (which ended up in tatters at the end of the night, because he kept biting at it). The older Canning boys had strict orders to keep the dog under control when the house was full of guests, which they did mostly by taking him outside and playing with him in the snow (which didn't help the big red bow around his neck much, either).

The house smelled wonderful, with that mixture of pine tree and warm cider and oranges and nutmeg and cinnamon and baked cookies and delicious sausages and other things rolled into pastries, which can really only mean one thing: a holiday party.

At seven o'clock, the first guests arrived. There was a tricky moment when Christopher's parents wanted to use his bedroom as a coat room. Christopher could only stutter, wondering what on earth he'd do with Gargoth, until Claire stepped in and offered her room instead. At eight o'clock, guests kept coming. By nine, the house was so full of people that they spilled out onto the front porch, laughing and eating and sipping delicious drinks despite the chilly night.

Cassandra was there, tall and slightly awkward but pleasant. She talked for a long time with the newspaper reporter, Stern, who lived a few houses down (he was ALMOST as tall as Cassandra). Whenever Christopher went near them, he overheard Stern saying things like, "... but we don't need more condos in the neighbourhood, what we really need are more parks ..." or, "... well, it was actually used to shelter exhausted horses ..." or, "... yes, a few of us are going to the city, a delegation...."

Christopher wasn't exactly sure what any of that meant, but it clearly meant a great deal to Stern and to Cassandra, who was listening intently beside the crackling fireplace.

Katherine and her parents were there. Hank and Marie Newberry were delighted to meet the family of Katherine's new best friend, and more delighted still to sneak up to the turret and say hello to their old friend, Gargoth.

When Marie Newberry peeked into Christopher's room, Gargoth could only stare at her, until she finally said, "Gargoth! Don't you remember me?" He didn't speak, only waddled toward her and waited patiently at her feet to be picked up. The little gargoyle sat on Marie's lap, silent and sad, as she spoke softly and gently stroked his wing. They were good friends.

She pulled a delicious-smelling apple from her purse and said, "It's from your tree in our backyard. It's still full of fruit." Gargoth took the apple without a word and put it in his pouch.

"I'd love to meet your friend, Ambergine," Marie said quietly. At the mention of Ambergine's name, though, Gargoth climbed back under the blankets in Christopher's messy chair and disappeared.

All evening, one of the friends kept an eye on Gargoth. Katherine and Christopher snuck upstairs to check on him a few times. Claire peeked in on him once and helped him re-tie her flowered scarf around his wing. But most of the evening Gargoth spent buried under the clothes of Christopher's chair.

Near midnight, Cassandra tore herself away from Stern and went to the top of the house to check on the gargoyle, coaxing him out from the pile of clothes with a mug of cocoa (a wintertime favourite of his).

As they were sitting quietly together, a knock came at the door. It opened slightly, and Stern entered the room.

Cassandra and Gargoth froze.

"Stern! Hi. This is Christopher's room, I'm just …" She floundered. There was nothing she could say. Stern's eyes were locked on the little gargoyle, frozen at her side.

Stern walked over and reached out. "He's … amazing … what a beautiful gargoyle," he whispered. He sounded like someone talking about a rare and ancient painting. Cassandra was stricken. She didn't know what to say. The reporter stroked the gargoyle.

"Yes," she said. "He's from the park. We rescued him." Cassandra frowned. For his part, Gargoth was doing a wonderful job of looking very much like a statue. He stared straight ahead and didn't flinch, statue-like.

"Rescued? Thank goodness. You saved him from the vandals?" Stern asked, his eyes still locked on the gargoyle.

"Yes, we saved him … he was kind of special, the nicest of the statues, and we found him untouched in the snow after the vandals left, so we brought him up here." Cassandra fidgeted. She wasn't much of a liar.

"He looks so real!" Stern reached forward and picked up the gargoyle. He stroked him and searched over his whole body.

"Oh! His wing! It's in tatters!" he exclaimed. "Too bad. He just seems so ... lifelike. He's amazing." He put the little gargoyle carefully on the desk, patted his head, then turned away (which is why he didn't see Gargoth stick his tongue out at him behind his back).

"I guess we should go back to the party?" Cassandra said, breathing out at last. The pair went back downstairs, but Cassandra knew a kindred spirit when she saw one: like Marie Newberry and a few other special adults, Stern-the-reporter loved Gargoth at first sight.

Chapter Thirty-four
The Balcony

It was late at night. Ambergine woke suddenly. The baby was crying nearby, again. She'd been in the cage in the kitchen for several weeks now, alone except whenever the Collector entered to bang one apple and one mug of water down on the table before her each morning. He always tormented her and placed them on the table just out of her reach, so she had to rock the cage dangerously to reach them.

Each night, he took a drink from the box with the food and the light inside. Ambergine had stopped surprising him in the dark, so he hadn't dropped any more drinks. Instead, she drew him into conversation.

Their conversations went something like this:

Ambergine: "You are up, again."

The Collector: "Don't speak to me."

Ambergine: "Do you have trouble sleeping?"

The Collector: "Shut up."

Ambergine: "I'm not surprised you can't sleep, with such guilt rattling around in your head."

The Collector: "Abomination! WHY DO YOU INSIST ON TORTURING ME?"

Then the furious old man would storm from the room, sometimes slapping her cage as he passed by, sometimes not. Then she would not see him again until the next night.

Ambergine counted the days by the rising and setting of the sun: she'd been locked in the cage almost a month. But there was another way to count the passage of time as well: the Cellini apple tree in the snowy backyard was growing at an astonishing rate. She knew the tree would be bearing fruit very soon, within a few days. It already stood as tall as a man.

She had been watching the neighbouring windows each night to keep her mind from wandering and to help her feel less lonely. People were definitely in a festive mood, and coloured lights had been appearing in nearby windows. A few nights earlier, she had watched an entire family in a house across the backyard gather around a piano and sing together for hours. It was odd watching them, since Ambergine could see them singing happily, but heard only silence locked in her dungeon of a cage.

And then last night, in one particular window a long way off … a light was shining on something that made her heart skip a beat. She had seen a boy with dark curly hair in that window a few times, and last night something else. A little figure which looked exactly like … but it couldn't be what she thought it was.

Could it?

She kept a very close eye on that window all day, now and then peering at the familiar object sitting in the windowsill, unsure if what she was seeing was real, or maybe she was just losing her mind. It was many windows away, quite a long distance off, so she couldn't see it clearly despite her excellent vision. She was more than a little worried that maybe she was hallucinating.

But it WAS a figure, a statue of *something*.

Just then the Collector entered the kitchen and poured his nightly drink. Ambergine went to work, as she had done every night.

Ambergine: "Can't you sleep?"

The old man turned and looked at her. She could see the light from the food box glinting off his thick glasses.

"Quiet, monster." He'd never called her that before.

Ambergine: "Monster? You're the one keeping me in a cage."

He was calmer this evening, and not to be baited. "You're a creature that shouldn't be, a mis-creation. Quite simply, a monster." He sipped his drink and turned to leave the kitchen.

Ambergine couldn't stop herself. "You're the monster. Didn't your mother love you, monster?" She said these last words so sweetly, so gently. She knew this was risky. Gargoth had told her that the Collector had lost his mother long ago, as a young boy.

With a sudden snarl, the old man smashed his cup on the floor. Ambergine drew back in her cage, frightened at the look on his face.

"How DARE YOU speak of her to me!" he whispered in the lowest, angriest hiss that Ambergine could ever imagine. He looked like a demon, with the half-light glinting off his thick glasses and his mouth curled in a wicked snarl. He stormed forward, threw open the window, and grabbed her cage. He gave it such a violent shake that she rattled inside it like a toy, and he drew his face up close to her.

"You will never see your precious Gargoth of Tallus, ever again!" he screamed. Then he tossed the cage out the window, where it pinwheeled through the air, end over end over end, landing with a thump in the snow. He slammed the window shut.

In the days to come, as other families in this story enjoyed holiday parties, delicious dinners, and companionship with loved ones, Ambergine lay cramped in her cage in the cold and dark of the snowy backyard.

Days passed, more snow fell, and she weakened.

Then everything went dark.

Chapter Thirty-five
A Candle Glows

Toronto was frozen under a cold January night sky, and the hard snow lay on the ground in trampled, icy mounds.

Katherine was sitting in Christopher's bedroom, looking down into the park.

A single candle was shining in the dark, in the spot where the apple tree once stood. It threw a weak, shimmery circle of light into the snow.

They were calling the Collector.

As the days drew into weeks, Christopher got more and more creepy notes in his mailbox. He noticed that with every new note, Cassandra grew somehow quiet and impatient at the same time. Finally, the day before, when he received yet another letter, Cassandra grew very quiet and said almost in a whisper, "Enough is enough. Here are some candles, go and stick them in the snow in the park tonight. It's time."

It was risky. But they really couldn't wait any longer — they had to do something.

The creepy notes were bad enough, but Gargoth was acting very odd as well. His wing was in tatters and he was still holding it up with Claire's flowery scarf (which was looking almost as dirty and bedraggled as his wing). He had also taken to hiding beneath Christopher's bed, which wasn't exactly the cleanest spot in the world. Gargoth seldom spoke, he barely crawled out from under the bed, and he had stopped eating. Occasionally, Claire could coax him out when she visited Christopher's room, but whenever she left he crawled back to his hiding spot.

And of course everyone was worried about Ambergine, but no one dared breathe her name in case Gargoth heard them and started to weep or gag or howl (all real possibilities). And poor Christopher flinched or broke into a sweat every time anyone mentioned her, too.

Everyone agreed that they had to call the Collector.

But how many nights did they have to leave the lit candle in the park? When was the Collector going to show up? What were they going to do when he did?

The two friends looked at the candle burning softly below them in the park. Normally Christopher would pick up his guitar and play his nightly serenade, but lately he didn't have the heart.

The park was too empty now.

Christopher had noticed that people came and went in the park, though. Since the vandalism, the city had often left the gates open, and with each passing day more and more people had slowly discovered the park. Neighbours sat on the benches by the fountain, eating their lunch. One older lady came by every afternoon with a basket of bread crumbs and fed the ever-present pigeons (Christopher wondered why *anyone* would want to feed such nasty birds). Two men played chess in the weak winter afternoon sun, the board propped between them on the bench. Parents pushed strollers with sleeping babies and sat for a few quiet moments by the seahorse fountain, which still bubbled away softly.

One regular visitor was a teenage boy with dark, curly hair.

Christopher had seen him again and again from his window as the winter days passed, sitting quietly by the fountain. He held something in his hand, a little figure, a statue maybe, which he rubbed absently with this thumb. Occasionally the teenager searched for something, looking into the skies or around the base of the bushes. Christopher was eventually curious enough about him to want to talk to him, and one day he went into the park to start a conversation (he'd been taking lessons from Claire). But by the time he got downstairs and through the gates, the teenager was gone.

The little seahorse fountain was still there. The bushes were still there. The park benches and flagstones were still there.

But it was just empty space to Christopher and Katherine.

For an entire week, the candle flickered in the snow of the park each night. Before he fell asleep,

Christopher snuck down and put it out, sometimes with Claire or Cassandra's help.

Christopher had also noticed that Cassandra was working awfully hard on something with Stern-the-reporter. He was often in Candles by Daye with loads of papers and neighbours coming and going.

The adults were clearly up to something of their own.

So the candle was lit and doused night after night, until one day Christopher found another handwritten envelope in the mailbox, with his name on it.

Inside was a letter which read: *"TOMORROW NIGHT, BRING THE CREATURE. NO TRICKS, OR ELSE."*

Chapter Thirty-Six
Of Statues and Trees

James was lying on his bed staring at the snowy sky, the little gargoyle statue in the window casting a shadow on the floor of his bedroom. His window was open a crack; he needed some fresh air to think clearly.

He had been back to the park again and again but saw nothing else. It was puzzling. He was sure he had discovered a gargoyle print in the snow by the fence on that first visit ... but all he had found there were broken statues and nothing since.

He was holding a letter from his grandfather. James had sent him photos of the park and the clipping from *The East End Crier* as soon as he discovered the gargoyle footprint weeks before, but his grandfather must not have received it yet; his letter didn't mention it. And James couldn't reach him by email, since his grandfather refused to use a computer. His grandfather's letter also said that he was leaving to go on holiday in Spain, and no one would be able to reach him for several months. So there was no point in phoning him, either.

James sighed. His grandfather had written to tell him about how the gargoyles were surviving the winter (their least favourite season).

Theodorus had decided to lie in a bathtub of warm water all winter long, his long arms drooping onto the tiled bathroom floor.

Septimus had taken to smoking his pipe by the fireplace for hours on end, telling stories to anyone who would listen (and often to those who didn't particularly want to hear).

Arabella was quiet and withdrawn and lived under the thatched eaves of the old cottage all winter long. She flew off as soon as night fell, then returned each morning.

James missed the gargoyles terribly. He missed his grandfather, too.

He went to close the window, brushed against Theodorus' gargoyle statue on the windowsill...

... and the statue fell out the window!

James gasped and grabbed for it, but missed. He watched in horror as the statue arced and spun through the air, landing in the deep snow of his backyard.

He dashed down the stairs and swung on his coat. He burst out the front door and banged into the garage, searching frantically for a snow shovel. In a few moments, he cleared off the snow along the walkway at the side of the house and made a path through the snow and to the backyard gate. He shovelled the snow non-stop until the gate was clear. Then he strode into the backyard to the spot where he'd seen the statue fall.

He didn't have to look too hard. The statue was resting in the soft snow, just below the surface. He found it quickly and was pocketing it when he heard a faint gravelly whisper at the very edge of his hearing: "Bellatro, groshen sawchen."

At the same time, he also heard the far-off whisperer say, "Boy ... an apple."

It sounded like the wind in the summer grass. It was an odd voice, a gravelly voice. And he had heard it before.

It was a *gargoyle's* voice!

He swivelled around, suddenly searching everywhere. His backyard was just his backyard. "Who ... who are you? Where are you?" he called. He had a short moment of panic as he wondered if he was hallucinating, hoping that his gargoyle statue wasn't talking to him from his pocket. He took it out and looked at it. No, it was just a statue.

"Who are you?" he called again.

There was silence. James grew frantic. He was sure he had heard a gargoyle's voice! He ran around the entire fence of his backyard. There was nothing there, just a few bushes. He stuck his head over the fence and peered into his neighbour's yard. He came face-to-face with an old dog tied up to a post, which wagged its tail at him.

"I don't think the dog is talking to me, unless I'm completely losing it," he said out loud.

"No. Here," said the soft voice again from far away, and weaker this time.

James whipped around. It came from several yards away, near the end of his street. He sprinted to the fence, placed a hand on it and vaulted over, landing in the soft snow on the other side with a thud. He vaulted fences, yard after yard, calling "Where are you?" as he went.

Suddenly he landed in a yard and came face-to-face with an apple tree, tall as a man, bursting out of the snow. It was bearing tiny apples.

It was very familiar.

"Where have I seen that apple tree before?" he said out loud. He ran toward it, then he remembered: it was the same kind of tree that he had seen in the little park with the gargoyle footprint in the snow. It was just like the tree that had been cut down!

James' heart started to pound. He looked frantically all around, but there was nothing to see, just snow ...

... then he saw it. There was a lump at the base of the tree, something partially covered with snow.

He ran over and fell on his knees, brushing madly at the snowy lump. He brushed until he uncovered a heavy iron cage, its door locked with an ancient padlock.

And inside was a *gargoyle*.

It looked like his carving, only softer. It looked a little like Theodorus and Septimus. It looked a lot like Arabella.

James stared in disbelief.

The gargoyle slowly opened its eyes and smiled weakly at him. It spoke in its whispery voice like the wind in the summer grass, but James understood it perfectly. "Your statue ... in the window ... I saw it fall...." The gargoyle paused and drew a slow, difficult breath.

"My statue? Yes!" James breathed. "You could see it?!"

"A gargoyle ..." it said gently again. Then the creature closed its eyes and slumped inside the cage, just as though it had died.

Chapter Thirty-Seven
The Big Event

Christopher's heart was thumping wildly. He didn't think he could find enough saliva in his mouth to speak, even if he wanted to.

He was standing knee deep in the snowy park, in the spot where the apple tree once stood. A lit candle wavered in the cold night air at his feet, which were slowly turning to blocks of ice. Katherine and Claire were hiding in the bushes with a cell phone, ready to call the police and tell them the vandal was in the park again. They had to leave Marbles in the house, since he couldn't be trusted to stay quiet in the bushes.

Cassandra was keeping a close eye on the park from her store across the street, waiting to join them as soon as the Collector arrived (there weren't THAT many bushes to hide behind in the park, and Cassandra was awfully tall to hide easily).

Christopher wished he had Cassandra and his big dog with him now.

Instead, beside him in the snow stood Gargoth, his head bowed, cradling his damaged wing in Claire's scarf. He was thin and grey and shivered as tears fell and froze in the snow at his taloned feet.

An eerie breeze blew by the two friends, embracing them both in dreary cold.

Christopher felt his heart squeeze. He couldn't bear to look at Gargoth. It seemed that he had watched his friend nearly vanish in the past few weeks. Without Ambergine, the little creature seemed completely lost and disinterested in the world around him.

Perhaps tonight they would set that right.

The sky was pitch black, the city quiet and too far away. He'd never felt so isolated, even though he was in the middle of a busy metropolis with thousands of people safe in their homes, all around him. His own home, his own family, was just steps away, but they might as well still be in Vancouver, he felt so far away from them.

"You okay, Gargoth?" Christopher finally mumbled. "When is he coming, do you think?"

The gargoyle stayed silent. He hadn't spoken much for many days. He seemed weary of everything.

The Collector was coming, for good or ill.

Just as Christopher thought he would scream with the tension of waiting, a man walked into the park. He appeared on the sidewalk and walked through the open gates. His feet crunched through the snow, and then there he was standing before them. He looked around then doused the light of the candle with one swift kick of snow.

Christopher and Gargoth stood before the Collector.

The little gargoyle made a strange noise in his throat, and Christopher wasn't sure if it was a growl or a whimper. Christopher felt that tiny lick of anger that had been surprising him lately. Oh, there was fear, but there was that little red hot point of rage, too.

"You've brought my property, I see. Good." The Collector reached out to grab Gargoth, but Christopher stepped between them.

"Where's Ambergine?" he demanded, surprising himself with his loud, steady voice.

The Collector sighed. "You're a fool, Christopher Canning. Did you really think I'd bring the other gargoyle along just for you to steal her from me, too?"

Christopher's eyes narrowed. Claire had said the Collector wouldn't bring Ambergine, and that they'd have to save her themselves. He couldn't loathe the man before him any more than he did at that moment. He actually felt his skin crawl, but he had to focus. He had a job to do. He could not fail his friend now.

Christopher drew a deep breath. "Okay. I can't stop you from taking him. But Gargoth has something to say to you, first."

The Collector laughed — he actually laughed — and said, "What could the creature possibly want to say to me? Go ahead, Gargoth. Do your little song and dance. Soon you'll be back where you belong in my mansion, and we'll put an end to all this escaping.

I broke the statues. I cut down the tree. Now I'm here to get you. You have no choice."

He said this in a slimy, heartless voice that made Christopher want to break his neck.

Gargoth lifted his weary face and looked the Collector in the eye. A thousand indignant, angry words sprang into Christopher's head, and he was about to shout them in the Collector's smug face … when Gargoth spoke.

"You couldn't be more wrong. I do have a choice," the gargoyle said quietly, but in a voice growing steady as a warming wind. The little creature raised his chin and his voice grew stronger.

"You may have stolen Ambergine, but she is not yours. You have tried to own me, but you do not. We will resist you always, at every turn, together and apart. And this is why you have lost: I *choose* not to be afraid of you anymore."

With that, many interesting things happened.

Suddenly the spotlight snapped on in Christopher's bedroom above them, brightly lighting the spot where they stood. Claire waved down at them from the window as the Collector snarled and whirled around to run. Christopher looked up at his window, bewildered. He had thought his sister was nearby in the bushes, calling for help. She must have snuck upstairs to his room during the long, cold wait.

But that's not all. At the moment the spotlight hit the snow, a loud bark came from the back door of Christopher's house and three large teenage boys burst outside, accompanied by a giant, bounding dog. Marc, Nathan, Adam, and Marbles tumbled and sprinted through the snow to the park gate, with much laughter and barking. The boys waved up at Claire in the window.

"Here, Claire?" Marc shouted up at her. She waved back and called, "That's perfect, right there!" No one in their right mind would try to run past those three, especially with Marbles leaping and whining as though he recognized the Collector and was eager for another shot at his pant leg.

Christopher heard a little bell tinkle, and saw the door of Candles by Daye fly open and then bang shut as Cassandra and Stern burst across the street to the park at a run. A moment later a police car pulled up to the park gates, siren wailing.

Then two more grown-ups walked into the park and waited quietly behind the teenage boys. They waved at Katherine, who stepped out from the bushes closing her cell phone. She had called her parents and they had arrived just in time to help. Gargoth's oldest Toronto friends, the Newberrys, were standing steadfast at the gates, too.

Katherine was also holding Stern's digital recorder, which she clicked off. She had just recorded everything the Collector had said, including the part where he admitted that he broke the statues and cut down the tree.

The Collector was trapped.

Christopher couldn't believe his eyes. A moment before he'd thought it was just him, Claire, Katherine, and the gargoyle in the park, and Cassandra across the street, waiting to stand up to the old man. But now there were seven other people there, including his giant, eager dog.

And a police officer was about to join them at any second. There was a perfect quiet moment before anything else happened, when even Marbles was still, and in that moment Katherine drew herself up close to the Collector and whispered in his face. "Gargoth doesn't belong to you, he never did and he never will. We saved him from you, for good."

Cassandra ran up, leaving Stern at the gates to talk with Katherine's parents. She managed to wheeze out, "We know you've got Ambergine, and we'll save her, too."

The Collector laughed a cruel, mean streak of a laugh. "You may think so, but you won't find her, I promise. It's too late for that!"

Then the police officer joined them in the spotlight.

Christopher looked up at his sister in the window. Claire must have got everyone to help without telling him so as not to worry him. She must have told Cassandra about the Collector and Ambergine, and together they made this foolproof plan to get everyone involved to help catch him.

Claire Canning wasn't one for keeping secrets, at least not the bad kind that let rotten people get away with things they shouldn't. He wanted to hug his sister at that moment, but instead he picked up the little gargoyle, who was silent and stiff as a statue in his arms.

"Let's go, Gargoth," Christopher whispered, and they quietly disappeared through the growing throng of people, back into the safety of Christopher's house and his bedroom turret. In the confusion no one saw them leave, and if anyone had heard Gargoth speak to his tormentor, well, unless they spoke his language, all they heard was the sound of the wind rustling in the winter leaves.

The park was a busy place all night. The police officer arrested the sullen Collector on the spot, right there in the snow, accompanied by much cheering from Christopher's brothers. The officer talked to Cassandra and Stern and was very interested to learn that the man being arrested was a visitor.

"We don't appreciate people cutting down city park trees," the officer told Cassandra. "And breaking statues, well that's just wrong. The judge will have lots of questions for him at the courthouse," he said as he led the old man away.

The last anyone saw of the Collector, he was head down in handcuffs, being led to a police car, dodging snowballs and an excited barking dog. There was a large crowd gathering from the neighbourhood, so anyone who cared to ask could know the truth: the park vandal had been caught, and he wasn't coming back.

A little gargoyle sat cradling his torn wing in a turret window high above the park, watching the goings-on down below all night long. The Collector was gone, Ambergine was lost, and somehow along the way, Gargoth of Tallus had found true friends.

Chapter Thirty-Eight
The Right Tool

James stood before the metal cage in his bedroom. It was a brutal thing, very old, with thick iron bars and a heavy padlock on the barred door. It had taken him some time to chip it out of the icy snow at the base of the tree and drag it back to his house as carefully as he could.

He had wrapped a blanket around the back of the cage and taken the space heater from his father's workshop in the garage, warming the room so it was almost too hot.

He couldn't imagine how to get the lock off the cage. He'd tried everything, including pouring wax into it to try to make an imprint of a key. He'd picked at it and fiddled with it for hours, but it just wouldn't open.

The only thing he hadn't done was take a hammer to it, but he didn't want to do that with the little creature inside.

And what a poor creature it was. After a few

hours in his room, he still wasn't able to tell if the gargoyle was alive or dead. He wished his grandfather was there; he would know what to do. He had called the old man in England as soon as he could, but there was no answer. He was still in Spain, on his winter holiday, and James had no way to contact him. He wished his grandfather would get over his distrust of computers. A quick email would mean everything right now.

The gargoyle was deathly still. Since he had dug its cage out of the snow, it hadn't moved or spoken. It was icy cold to the touch, and its wings were frozen solid, like stone.

What was it doing in Toronto? What was it doing in a cage in the snow? What if it *hadn't* seen Theodorus's statue fall from his window and called out for help?

James had a lot of questions, but he had to put them aside as he focused on the task before him.

He had picked all the tiny apples from the golden tree, and they were resting in a basket at the side of the cage. He'd had an odd moment as he collected the fruit. After he'd picked the last sweet apple from its branches, the little tree had toppled over into the snow, turned black and shrivelled up, dead. He stared at it, hoping with all his heart that it wasn't the bad omen it seemed.

He warmed a jug of water, in case the creature should wake and want a drink. He wished he'd asked his grandfather a lot more questions about gargoyles all summer long.

He had done everything he could think of to make the gargoyle comfortable.

Except free it from the cage.

James sighed and turned back to the problem of the padlock. Whether the gargoyle lived or died, he was going to get it out of the cage. He bent his head patiently to the task, picking again and again at the rusty lock.

He would remain at his task all night if need be.

At midnight a gentle knock came at his door, and his father peered into the room. James jumped and tried to cover the cage, but his father had already seen what lay within.

His father took a few steps into the room and James started rambling, terribly close to tears.

"It's a gargoyle. I found it in the snow in a yard way down the street. I need to get it out of this cage, but I don't know how...."

His father rolled up his sleeves and looked thoughtfully into the cage for a few moments. He didn't seem overly surprised by what he saw. He scratched his head then said, "A gargoyle statue, huh? Does it mean that much to you? Okay. Didn't your grandfather give you a bag of stonemason's tools? The chisel and saws might work. They cut stone, don't they?"

James looked at his father in surprise. "And metal?" he whispered.

His father nodded and scratched his head again. "Maybe. If we do it together, we might be able to pry one of these old bars out of the base. That one's pretty rusty. But why do you care so much about an old gargoyle statue?"

James ignored him and flew into the basement, digging frantically through piles of laundry, old boots, and magazines, to the back of the storeroom where he'd carelessly tossed his grandfather's stone-cutting tools.

The golden letters and symbols glinted as James's hand found the ancient leather bag in the dark.

CHAPTER THIRTY-NINE
THE PARK RISES

The winter holiday ended. Katherine and Christopher went back to school, inseparable, sitting together in every class and spending most evenings together at Candles by Daye, doing their homework.

But each day before nightfall, they toured the city for any sign of Ambergine. They covered park after park, they went through backyards and school playgrounds, they looked high and low for their lost friend.

Christopher didn't have to keep his secret anymore. It was such a relief when he told Katherine that the Collector had stolen Ambergine. Katherine didn't stay too mad for too long. She understood how much it had cost Christopher to keep the secret from her.

The Collector was gone. No one knew where he had lived when he sat watching from the library rooftop all those long months. Stern had done some snooping, but no one could find the old man's last known address.

Where could Ambergine be? The friends were not going to give up on her, but it was hard to keep looking without any clues.

Gargoth lived quietly in Christopher's or Claire's room, or at Candles by Daye. He spoke little and ate less, although he did sometimes curl up on Katherine's knee, or Claire's. He still had her flowery scarf, which was now barely more than a tattered rag, just like his wing.

As winter turned to spring there was some amazing news, though. Stern and Cassandra had managed to do some magic of their own.

One afternoon Christopher and Katherine were doing homework together in his room. He was looking out his bedroom window into the little park (which he now did very rarely) and was surprised to see city workers there. He sat on the window seat and watched with interest.

It was a slushy March day, and warming air blew over the old snow tops and ice burrows of the park. City workers in bright vests were cleaning out the fountain and two more were unwrapping a new park bench. Now there were three benches in a nice circle around the fountain.

"That'll make the pigeon lady happy," Christopher said out loud.

"What will?" Katherine asked, joining him at the window.

Another worker used a hand truck to position a heavy-looking box. They watched with interest as he wrestled the box into place then tore it open to reveal a new stone chess table.

"Those two chess-playing men will like that, too," Christopher said.

One worker stood off by himself, pounding a metal stake into the ground. It had a sign on it. Christopher and Katherine decided they had to see what was going on and went downstairs, grabbing Marbles on the way. As they approached the park, they saw Cassandra and Stern standing at the park gates.

Cassandra waved. "It's amazing! Come quick!"

They ran over and Katherine read the signpost out loud:

> *Gatepost Park, Established 1904. This Toronto Heritage Park first opened to the public in 1904, the year of the Great Toronto Fire. Its fence and fountain harboured many of the exhausted horses used to pull ladder-and-pump wagons during that terrible night. As a heritage site, its gates will remain open, inviting the people of Toronto to enjoy its peaceful space, always.*

"Stern did it, well, most of it," Cassandra said. The adults looked happily at each other. "And he's writing an article about it in *The East End Crier*. It's official, the park stays. And look." Cassandra pointed at the gateposts, where two new gargoyle statues perched looking out over the street. They were made of stone and had wise and solemn faces.

"So there will always be gargoyles here," she whispered, gently squeezing Christopher's shoulder. They weren't Gargoth and Ambergine, but Christopher understood. It was an homage to his friends, even though one seemed lost forever.

From that day on, the park was well used. Neighbours came and sat on the benches feeding pigeons or playing chess. Families sat around the fountain enjoying the warmer spring weather, and children played in the space where the apple tree once stood. Shop clerks and store owners unwrapped their lunches and drank their tea on the benches. The park became a busy space that everyone in the neighbourhood loved.

Christopher found he didn't really want to go into the park, though.

Then one day a warmer wind blew and spring arrived for good. The tops of the frozen snow banks melted, and almost overnight the city gave itself to light and sun.

That was the day the teenage boy with the dark, curly hair visited the park again, the boy Christopher had noticed sitting on the snowy benches so often after the park was first vandalized.

And this time he wasn't alone.

The boy had an old man with him. The man was wearing a bizarre bright green cloak and a huge, floppy matching green hat, and carried a large leather bag.

Christopher watched them closely from his window.

There was something about the old man and the teenager that made Christopher watch with interest (apart from the old man's odd clothes). Unlike most visitors to the park, they didn't unwrap any food, or pull out chess pieces, or try to feed the foul pigeons.

Instead, the old man pulled out a magnifying glass and began carefully looking in the muddy grass along the fence.

What could he *possibly* be looking for?

The teenage boy did a most unusual thing as well. He looked around to see if anyone was watching (although he didn't notice Christopher in the turret window high above him), then he pulled a small figure out of his shirt pocket and rubbed its head. He brought the figure to his lips, then put it back in his pocket.

Next he opened the large leather bag at his feet, took out a statue, and placed it beside him on the bench.

Except it wasn't a statue.

It was a *gargoyle*! And she looked *awfully* familiar!

The little creature slowly shuffled on the bench, tired and weak, wings hanging in tatters.

Christopher choked. He started coughing his head off and pointing. He couldn't speak. He tried to call out, but all he could do was squeak.

He ran down the stairs and burst into Claire's room. She wasn't there. He dove onto his knees and looked under her bed, but Gargoth wasn't there either, which was odd. The gargoyle never left his spot under her bed unless it was to visit Christopher in his turret or Cassandra in Candles by Daye.

Christopher flew downstairs and out the front door. He whipped into the park and screeched to a halt, chest heaving.

The park was empty.

He ran around the entire park, his head whipping from side to side, but the old man, the teenager and the gargoyle had vanished.

Where? Where could they have gone?

A bell tinkled across the street, and he caught the corner of a bright green cape as the door to Candles by Daye closed behind it. He waited forever to get safely through traffic and across the street to Cassandra's store …

… where he opened the door to a most amazing scene.

The old man in the green cloak and floppy green hat was standing beside Cassandra, who had her arm around Katherine's shoulders, who was standing beside Claire, who stood beside the boy with dark, curly hair. The boy fiddled with a small statue in his hand: it *was* a little gargoyle, and it looked a lot like Gargoth.

The old man was introducing himself, his bright green hat wobbling as he talked excitedly and pumped Cassandra's hand.

"When she knew where she was, the gargoyle kept pointing at your store! I'm Gregory, by the way, and this is my grandson James."

Everyone had animated, silent faces, as though important things were happening in slow motion.

"My name is Tallus. I'm Gregory Tallus.…"

Tallus? TALLUS? The named screamed inside Christopher's head, but no one was really listening to the old man.

Instead they were all looking at the countertop, where two tattered gargoyles stood face to face (one with his wing in the rags of a flowered scarf), tears plopping and hissing at their feet.

Christopher's eyes fell upon the old leather bag beside the gargoyles. It had the initials "G.T." in gold lettering: Gregory Tallus. Then Christopher's eyes rested on a golden symbol stamped into the leather beside the letters.

It was an odd symbol that Christopher knew well and set his heart thumping.

It was a stonemason's mark, a circle with two diamonds inside:

Chapter Forty
The Almost Very End of the Story

A few days after their meeting in Candles by Daye, Gregory Tallus and his grandson James gathered everyone in the park. It was a beautiful spring day, sunny and warm without being too hot. No one else was in the park, so everyone sat on the park benches around the bubbling fountain. The bushes were starting to turn green and leafy again, so the little crowd was out of sight of the street.

Cassandra and Stern sat happily on one bench together (it slowly dawned on Christopher that perhaps Cassandra and Stern were meant for each other). Christopher, Katherine, and her parents sat on another bench, and Claire and James (who had discovered that they were in the same high school chemistry class) sat together on the third. The gargoyles were there too, resting in the huge leather bag that Gregory Tallus carried with him.

Gregory had switched his cape to bright purple today, but he kept the green, floppy hat. Katherine found him astonishing and couldn't take her eyes off him.

After saying hello to everyone, he took a long sip of mint tea from a thermos he carried with him under his cloak. He cleared his throat (which Christopher thought sounded very theatrical) and began. "My friends. It is remarkable, astonishing, that we are here today, in the presence of these two wondrous creatures. Two gargoyles we only supposed *might* exist...."

"*We?*" a chorus of voices asked. Everyone on the benches had a lot of questions ... and Gregory had promised he would answer them all, but he hadn't told them much until now.

"Yes, we, the Tallus family. I'm the last Tallus by name ... James has his father's last name. Our ancestor was the French stonemason Tallus, who was a gifted sculptor and created many gargoyles in his lifetime. Here is his symbol: the circle with two diamonds inside, one on top of the other. As you know, his gargoyles carry his mark." Gregory pointed at the golden symbol on his leather bag.

"Tallus died in England over four hundred years ago, but his family has always known about his gargoyles, and we have searched for them for hundreds of years. Gargoth, Ambergine, and the others in England...."

"OTHERS?" Katherine's mother and Cassandra said together, rather loudly.

James broke in then. "My grandfather is trying to say that Gargoth and Ambergine aren't alone. There are more gargoyles like them in the world, three more, in fact."

The friends sitting around the benches all looked at each other.

More gargoyles? Like Gargoth and Ambergine?

James went on. "My grandfather has known the other gargoyles and cared for them all his life. I met them this summer, and one of them, Theodorus, made me this statue."

Theodorus?

James took the statue from Theodorus out of his pocket and handed it to Claire, who studied it with care. It looked almost exactly like Gargoth. She passed it along for the others to see.

Gregory Tallus continued. "Tallus hid his gargoyles well, to keep them safe. He hid them in lonely churchyards in out-of-the-way little towns, some in France, one in England.

"For generations Tallus family members quietly talked to villagers and listened to old stories and folk tales about creatures living in churchyards. We travelled throughout France and England and scoured newspapers and journals until my great-great-great grandfather and his granddaughter found Septimus. She and her grandson found Theodorus, then finally, my grandfather found Arabella. And in turn, my grandson James found Ambergine a few months ago … and she led us to Candles by Daye and to Gargoth."

The friends on the benches all sat stock still and listened intently, looking much like a group of statues themselves. Gregory took another sip of tea and continued:

"The Tallus family has created a sanctuary for the gargoyles in a garden in England. There is water and apple trees and ponds. The three gargoyles there have a safe place to live together if they want, though they are free to come and go as they please.

"The garden is far from any towns, far from any roads, there is no one who knows about it other than those whom we tell, and those are very few indeed. And now we are telling you, the friends and protectors of Gargoth and Ambergine. You are all welcome to the garden."

There was a gentle murmur. Cassandra cleared her throat. "Mr. Tallus, that's a wonderful invitation and I would love to meet the gargoyles living there. But what about Gargoth and Ambergine?" she asked.

The old man smiled. "Yes, Ms. Daye. I'm getting to that. You have, of course, noticed that Ambergine is very unwell. Her trauma in the snow before James found her, well, it has weakened her considerably. She cannot speak, she is partly blind, her wings were frozen solid. Over the centuries, my family has learned many secrets for restoring gargoyles to good health. I can help her regain her voice and her sight, and I can ease the pain of her frozen wings, which will heal in time. Gargoth's wing will heal, also, with the right care. I'm sure they will both fly again, sooner than you think. But they will need my help to do so.

"That is why Ambergine and Gargoth are invited to come to the English garden. They have agreed. They will meet Theodorus, Septimus, and Arabella. They will have company and safety, and good health that they can't find here. So you can take some comfort in this news, here are pictures and my journal, all about the gargoyles and the garden."

Gregory reached into the leather bag and pulled out papers, photographs, and a heavy journal, which he passed out among the friends.

Katherine was holding a photograph of a naughty-looking gargoyle smoking a pipe. A name was written in the space at the bottom of the photograph: Septimus of Tallus. He reminded her a great deal of Gargoth, and she couldn't help it. Tears sprang to her eyes.

"But the Collector is gone! The park is saved!" she blurted out. "They ARE safe here! We CAN keep them safe now!" Katherine's mother put her arm around her daughter.

Gregory Tallus nodded. "I know you don't want to say goodbye to them. You don't have to. They'll be there, in the garden. You'll know where to find them. And they could come back one day, when they are ready."

The group of friends was very quiet for a long while, looking at the photographs and the journal that Gregory had handed around. The journal was a heavy, leather-bound book with pages and pages of notes and stories about the gargoyles. It had gold letters on the cover and was titled "The

Gargoyle of Tallus," because as Gregory explained, when the journal was started by his great-great-great grandfather, there was only Septimus in the garden.

Katherine's mother was turning the pages and looking with wonder at all the gargoyle statues and notes Gregory Tallus and his family had made.

James was murmuring in Claire's ear, and she laughed out loud. They were looking at a photograph of a large, dark gargoyle with a ram's head and curly horns. Christopher could see the name, Theodorus of Tallus, written underneath the photograph, and the big gargoyle looked like he was laughing.

That was something that Christopher suddenly longed to hear: a laughing gargoyle. He knew Ambergine and Gargoth well, but he had never heard them laugh. Why not?

At that moment, Katherine passed along another photo: Arabella of Tallus. This gargoyle was clearly a girl, smaller than the other two, and she looked a lot like Ambergine but a little sadder.

Here was proof of three more living gargoyles, all similar to Ambergine and Gargoth, yet all three somehow different, too.

Christopher wanted to ask a burning question that had been on his mind since the moment he met Cassandra and the gargoyles in the park that night, so long ago. He cleared his throat and tried not to let his voice sound sad (although he had noticed that since the night in the snow with Gargoth and the Collector, his voice seemed older and stronger).

"I have a question. Can you tell us why the gargoyles are alive? I mean, why they aren't just statues? How did Tallus, your ancestor, do that?" He looked around. He realized by the looks on everyone's faces that they had all been wondering the same thing, but no one wanted to ask. It seemed almost rude, a bit like asking about where babies came from or how people felt about religion.

But Gregory Tallus nodded again (which made his bizarre green hat wobble dangerously). "Ah, yes. At some point we've all wondered that, Christopher." The old man looked at him kindly and smiled.

"I can tell you that each of the gargoyles was created in a churchyard, and each was carved freely, meaning they weren't part of a building or anything else. They were all carved from a single, freestanding piece of stone, probably a leftover from a restoration that Tallus was working on. All five have the same stonemason's mark: a circle with two diamonds inside it.

"But I've often wondered myself how, exactly, a lump of stone comes to life? I don't know the answer to that, honestly. Perhaps the simple love and care that Tallus gave his creations was enough? A spark of love, or joy, or individuality that the artist gave to his statues as he laboured over them and created them. That's what creation is, after all, isn't it? A passage of something special and personal from creator to creation?

"Or perhaps it was the gargoyles themselves who wanted to come to life. Who knows? The magic of their existence will remain a beautiful unsolved mystery, for all time."

The friends were silent for a long while considering this answer, then Cassandra spoke. "There are just five gargoyles then? For sure?" she asked, almost wistful.

Gregory grew thoughtful and frowned. "I believe so ... if there are others then they were so well hidden by Tallus that they are probably gone forever. But these two gargoyles appeared in the most unexpected way, so one never knows, I suppose."

He took another sip of tea from his thermos and smiled at the group before him. It seemed that something final had been said, and an end was drawing closer.

"And now, Gargoth has something he wants to say to each of you." The old man lifted Gargoth gently out of the bag, then Ambergine after him.

Gargoth took Ambergine by the claw and the two creatures waddled around the benches, from friend to friend. When Gargoth took Christopher's hand in his claw and said, "Thank you for all the beautiful music, Christopher Canning, I will always think of you whenever I hear a guitar," Christopher's eyes grew blurry and his glasses steamed up, so all he could do was nod. But no one seemed to notice, and he found he didn't even mind that much.

Katherine and her parents were the last to say goodbye. Katherine's mother held Gargoth the longest, and had the hardest time putting him down. She put something in his claw as she did.

"It's an apple, Gargoth, from the tree in our garden. The last Cellini apple tree in Toronto, maybe anywhere, from the tree you grew when you first came to us."

Gargoth looked a long time at the apple in his claw, then back at Katherine's mother. "I'm glad I followed you home so long ago. I'm glad I chose you, Mother Newberry," he said simply.

Then Gargoth led Ambergine to the spot in the park where the apple tree once stood, and the gargoyles planted the apple in the soil together.

They were going to the English garden to meet Theodorus, Septimus, and Arabella, to a life of good health, safety, and comfort. You should know that they both heal and fly once again. You might also like to know that despite some gentle bickering between Gargoth and Septimus about who tells the best stories, they all get along quite well.

Their old friends will visit them now and then. They will see Katherine and her parents, and Cassandra Daye and Stern-the-reporter. James will visit his grandfather and the gargoyles every summer, and eventually his friends Claire and Christopher Canning will visit, too.

It may be a little while before you see them again, though. Oh, they'll continue to have adventures, but quiet ones which they'll keep to themselves, at least for now.

Still, if you ever find Gatepost Park in downtown Toronto, say hello to the gargoyles at the gates, then sit and let the fence and fountain harbour you. You'll find a glorious apple tree waiting for you, in all seasons.

EPILOGUE

Think well into the future, past the time when young children have grown to become grandparents. It is a beautiful summer day, and you are standing looking at an English church. It's an ancient place, hundreds and hundreds of years old, with a little stream running beside the courtyard and a small apple orchard nearby. It is quiet, quiet, and the wind gently blows the leaves in the trees.

You let your eyes pass over the lion statue with its left ear broken off, the piece lying still in the grass at the statue's feet. You may lift the piece and fit it perfectly onto the lion's broken ear, where it will perch until wind and time topples it again. You see the old church walls and the ivy clinging to the sides of the ancient stones.

You will likely see (because you are curious and can still hear the language in the rustling winter leaves) the outline of a wing and a leathery head chasing through the ivy. You will hear a trill of laughter and look on in amazement as an apple core lands at your feet. There is something here that you can't quite name, but you DO know without being told that this is a place of stories, a place of friendship and magic.

Because that's really what this story is all about.

You have followed them from the very beginning, and by now you know the truth off by heart: somewhere, maybe closer than you think, a gargoyle waits.

ACKNOWLEDGEMENTS

Thank you to Allister Thompson, my wonderful editor, and to Emma Dolan for capturing the right tone with her talented illustration and design. Also special thanks to Sylvia McConnell for setting me on the path, and to the good folks at Dundurn for the continued wisdom and support. Finally, thanks to Paul and Ben for living so well with a writer, and an extra hug to Sarah, who first told me to write it all down.

A NOTE FROM THE AUTHOR

Gargoyles are all around. You'll find them on buildings, churches, and even see them as ornaments in people's yards. The gargoyle pictured here visits my own yard, now and then.

THE LOST GARGOYLE SERIES

The Gargoyle in My Yard
978-1894917827
$9.99

What do you do when a 400-year-old gargoyle moves into your backyard? Especially when no one else but you knows he's ALIVE? Twelve-year-old Katherine Newberry can tell you all about life with a gargoyle. He's naughty. He gets people into trouble. He howls at the moon, breaks statues, and tramples flowers to bits, all the while making it look like you did it! He likes to throw apple cores and stick his tongue out at people when they aren't looking. How do you get rid of a gargoyle? Do you help the gargoyle leave for good? If you're like Katherine and her parents, after getting to know him, you might really want him to stay.

A SYRCA Diamond Willow nominee

A Canadian Children's Book Centre Best Book

A SILVER BIRCH EXPRESS NOMINEE

The Gargoyle Overhead
978-1926607030
$9.95

It's not always easy, but thirteen-year-old Katherine Newberry is friends with a gargoyle. His name is Gargoth of Tallus, and he lives in her backyard. Gargoth has lost the only creature on the planet who can help him. Her name is Ambergine, and she's been his greatest friend for hundreds of years. What Katherine and Gargoth don't know is that Ambergine is searching for him too. But she is not alone. Gargoth's greatest enemy, The Collector, is prowling the city, and it's a race against time to find him first! This sequel to *The Gargoyle in My Yard* provides the historical backstory to Gargoth's life, and further explores themes of friendship, courage, and loneliness.

 **DUNDURN**
www.dundurn.com

Visit us at
Dundurn.com
Definingcanada.ca
@dundurnpress
Facebook.com/dundurnpress